Mary Harriott Norris

Henry Wadsworth Longfellow's Evangeline

A Tale of Acadie

Mary Harriott Norris

Henry Wadsworth Longfellow's Evangeline
A Tale of Acadie

ISBN/EAN: 9783337246624

Printed in Europe, USA, Canada, Australia, Japan

Cover: Foto ©Andreas Hilbeck / pixelio.de

More available books at **www.hansebooks.com**

The Students' Series of English Classics.

HENRY WADSWORTH LONGFELLOW'S
EVANGELINE
A Tale of Acadie

EDITED,

WITH INTRODUCTION AND NOTES,

BY

MARY HARRIOTT NORRIS

PROFESSOR OF ENGLISH LITERATURE, NEW YORK CITY

EDITOR OF GEORGE ELIOT'S "SILAS MARNER" AND SIR WALTER SCOTT'S
"MARMION"

AUTHOR OF "DOROTHY DELAFIELD," "THE NINE BLESSINGS," "JOHN APPLE-
GATE, SURGEON," "LAKEWOOD: A STORY OF TO-DAY," ETC.

LEACH, SHEWELL, & SANBORN,

BOSTON. NEW YORK. CHICAGO.

PREFACE.

Some knowledge of Henry Wadsworth Longfellow as scholar and poet is necessary to the equipment of any one desirous of possessing a general acquaintance with the development of English literature in the United States.

The editor of *Evangeline* therefore has made a direct effort in her Notes and Introduction to keep this twofold need in mind. To facilitate her purpose she has deemed it her duty, rather than that of the pupil, to supply most of the knowledge obtainable from dictionaries and cyclopædias. Moreover, it is no help to a student, eager for information, but destitute of library or works of reference, or greatly limited in time, to be told to consult dictionary or cyclopædia. If he has average intelligence, he knows as much as this himself.

The editor occasionally has made a digression in her annotations on words like "emblazon" or "ambrosial," which, while really giving information extraneous to the subject-matter, nevertheless afford an opportunity better to judge of Longfellow's culture, and its importance as a factor in his final poetic expression. By tracing the source of many of the poet's allusions, she has tried to emphasize the value of varied reading as an element of

iii

literary power. It is her earnest hope that students will be inspired to devote the time she has attempted to save for them in a closer examination than they might otherwise have made of peculiarities of style and construction, and of the principles of poetics.

The purity of thought and feeling embodied in *Evangeline* are worthy of a month of study; for in this narrative poem Longfellow has caught the true spirit of the gleeman, the minnesinger, the *trouvère,* — a spirit of graphic yet tender recital, mingled with deft reflection.

MARY HARRIOTT NORRIS.

New York, *April*, 1896.

CONTENTS.

INTRODUCTION.

When we consider that since the invention of printing till early in the nineteenth century, about eleven million volumes have been issued, and that five thousand of these have been written on Goethe alone, we gain a fresh idea of the importance of the few writers whose names and works become pre-eminent. Among the favored few stands Henry Wadsworth Longfellow.

A writer in the January *Forum* of 1893 made the statement that at one time a literature of genius was produced in America, although the greater portion appeared in Massachusetts. He named as men of genius, Whittier, Bryant, Hawthorne, Poe, Emerson, Irving, Prescott, Motley, Lowell, Holmes, and Longfellow, all of whom were born between 1780 and 1825. Since 1825, this writer further stated, no author has arisen in the United States who can be compared with these men. The reason given for this literary peculiarity was that by 1780 the people of Massachusetts especially, who were of English stock, had become homogeneous, and had then begun to develop a "literature of power" in poetry, romance, oratory, philosophy, history, and theology.

Whatever may be our opinion of the justness of such a limitation of genius in letters in the United States, of one thing we are assured; among these notable men, Henry Wadsworth Longfellow is the representative poet. It will be an interest-

1

ing task to see whether he was in ancestry, in his moral, intellectual, and social development, and also in the form and content of his poetic expression, a typical American.

The poet was of pure English stock, as his maternal ancestors, the Wadsworths, as well as the Longfellows, came from Yorkshire. On his mother's side he was descended from "John Alden and Priscilla," while on his father's side his progenitors showed that evolution of an American family before our Civil War which produced a "gentleman" whom Piers the Ploughman could have accepted, and such a man of the world and of affairs as polite society everywhere welcomes.

Longfellow the poet was the son of Stephen Longfellow, lawyer and statesman. The lawyer was the son of a farmer, who was also judge of the Court of Common Pleas. The farmer was the son of a blacksmith. The blacksmith was the possible prototype of Basil in *Evangeline;* he was also in the thought of the poet when writing : —

> "Thanks, thanks to thee, my worthy friend,
> For the lesson thou hast taught!
> Thus at the flaming forge of life
> Our fortunes must be wrought;
> Thus on its sounding anvil shaped
> Each burning deed and thought!"
>
> [See poem, *The Village Blacksmith.*]

A praiseworthy effort is now being made to preserve the birthplaces or the sometime dwellings of famous Americans. But before this sensible thought had seized the national mind, the fine old home of Captain Samuel Stephenson, in Portland, Me., where Henry Wadsworth Longfellow was born, Feb. 27, 1807, was converted into a tenement. Its dignified front, instead of commanding Casco Bay, as it did early in the century, now faces a mass of railway buildings. However, the brick house where the poet's youth was passed still exists in the very centre of the business portion of Maine's chief town. This house was the property of Longfellow's maternal grandfather, General Peleg Wadsworth, who also owned an extensive tract of land known as the Wadsworth Grant. Between this estate and the farm of his paternal grandfather at Gorham, the future poet had a fine range of country life in his summer vacations.

While sensitively organized, he grew to manhood well balanced in body, mind, and temperament. His instincts and habits were orderly, and his impulses upright.

By means of his father's small but well-selected library, the Portland library, and the bookstore of a Mr. Johnson, the boy had a chance to feed his literary instincts, which had a rapid, but by no means precocious, development.

His school-life began at three, and, including his professorships, ended at forty-seven.

At six years of age he could read, spell, and multiply. At seven he had gone half through the Latin grammar. His first poem, *The Battle of Lovell's Pond*, was written when he was thirteen, and published in the *Portland Gazette*. It was an imitative ballad, and is of no importance except to show a certain youthful impressionability to rhyme and rhythm.

At fourteen Longfellow passed the entrance examinations for Bowdoin, graduating from that college in 1825. Nathaniel Hawthorne was one of several classmates who rose to distinction. During his college-life Longfellow dabbled in poetry; but only five of the poems written at that time found a place in his first volume of original poetry, *Voices of the Night*, published in 1839.

Bryant was his first master. The simplicity, dignity, and blank verse of Bryant no doubt helped clarify both the thought and style of one who, all his life, was dominated by the Latin races in his persistent use of rhyme.

At seventeen his literary ambitions were clearly defined, and his letters to his father at this time are interesting in affording a glimpse of his estimate of himself. His father's replies are characteristic of the early part of this century, the point of view of an American gentleman, and of the healthful relation existing between father and son.

But circumstances as well as natural proclivity helped shape Longfellow's future course. He did not blaze his way to fame. In his case, as in that of Wordsworth, a series of events led to such a simple and natural evolution of the poet that his literary development seemed inevitable. He most earnestly desired, after graduation from Bowdoin, to spend a year at Cambridge; and this wish, through the indulgent co-operation of his father, he was enabled to gratify. In these days of heavy college expenses, it is interesting to note that the cost of a year at Cambridge in 1825 was about $184.

The poet's career as a man was destined, however, to a most auspicious beginning; for the Board of Trustees of Bowdoin voted, at the Commencement in 1825, to establish a " Professorship of the Modern Languages." The Board proposed that Henry W. Longfellow should visit Europe to further fit himself in languages, and that on his return the chair should be his.

Although Longfellow was versatile and talented, he realized, after his arrival in France, that long and varied post-graduate study was essential for a thorough professional equipment. An absence from home of three years, during which he had studied in France, Spain, Italy, and Germany, greatly broadened his views, deepened his perceptions, and admirably fitted him to inspire his pupils with true ideas of literary culture, and to disabuse their minds of the notion that the acquisition of a language is the easy pastime of a few lessons, or that education, much less culture, is the possession of a mass of unassimilated and heterogeneous information.

His arrival in America, in August, 1829, was followed the next month by his return to Bowdoin in the double capacity of professor and librarian, at a salary of one thousand dollars. He remained five and a half years, teaching, editing text-books for his pupils, and lecturing. He also, in 1831, began to write for the *North American Review*, his first paper in that periodical being entitled " The Origin and Progress of the French Language." His articles for the *New England Magazine* bore the appropriate title of " The Schoolmaster," and eventually were revised and incorporated in *Outre-Mer*, his first prose work, which was published in 1835. His first book, however, was a small volume of ninety pages of translations from the Spanish, published in 1833.

His nomination to the " Smith Professorship of Modern Languages " in Harvard University in 1834 led to a second preliminary journey abroad for purposes of study both in German and in the Scandinavian tongues.

The summer of 1835 was spent in Stockholm, studying Swedish and Finnish. In September he was in Copenhagen, pursuing Icelandic and Danish. October found him in Holland, acquiring Dutch. In December he reached Heidelberg, where he began a thorough course of German literature. As in his translation of *The Children of the Lord's Supper* we have a memento of his life in Sweden, so in *Hyperion*, his second prose work, published in 1839, do we trace the course of his contact with German sentiment.

Probably no American professor of languages in 1837 had so thorough an equipment as Longfellow.

It is the knowledge of his protracted study of languages, his
life-long association with the New England literati, his resi-
dence at Cambridge, his lectures at Harvard and his public.
lectures, his many translations, notably that of the *Divine
Comedy*, added to the general air of books, travel, culture, and
great personal refinement investing him during the entire period of manhood, which makes it so difficult to distinguish how
much of his success in life was due to culture, how much to
talent, and whether his talent at times passed its boundary,
and sought the rarer atmosphere of genius.

Certainly, if one should attempt to place Longfellow's poetry
under any one division, it would be that of sentiment. He
never became the exponent of absolute passion as did Shelley,
Keats, and Mrs. Browning. He failed to reach, in *Evangeline*,
those heights of feeling attained by Tennyson in *Guinevere*
and *Elaine*. Again, he was under no pressure of time and
place to exert himself outside the realm of translation, lyrics,
and narratives; for he was the dove sent out of the ark of his
country's intelligence, and he returned bearing a twig of Old
World culture and lore. By his American tact, instinct, and
religiousness, he vivified the mass of European material he had
assimilated with a warmth of national color and tone and thus
rendered it acceptable, when a poet with the outfit of a Landor
or a Swinburne would have been silenced by stern Puritan dis-
approval. He was the conspicuous forerunner of American
cosmopolitanism in letters. At the same time, there is much
that Longfellow has written which could not be fully appre-
ciated outside of English-speaking peoples. Who, besides the
English and Americans, could understand Elizabeth's spiritual sophistication in *The Theologian's Tale?* Her love is so
quaintly, and withal naturally, expressed that we listen with
the hero's devout and sympathetic ear to her confession.

In passing, it is interesting to compare the hexameter of *The Theologian's Tale* with that of *Evangeline;* it is much more unevenly written, often degenerating into prose, as does also that of the otherwise beautiful version of Bishop Tegnér's *The Children of the Lord's Supper.*

The setting of *The Birds of Killingworth*, as well as of *The Courtship of Miles Standish* and of *Hiawatha*, is distinctly national. Notwithstanding these and kindred poems, Longfellow has been called the least American of our poets. His versatility and responsiveness were great; but he was thoroughly American, while at the same time as much a reflector of European poetry as Chaucer was of the Italian Renaissance poetry. He was by turns a Spaniard, an Italian, a German, and a Scandinavian in thought, a Frenchman in diction, but always an American in omnivorousness of acquisition and selection, and supremely what might be called an indigenous product of Puritanism in nineteenth century New England transition.

Heine's influence is seen in *The Day is Done, Twilight,* and *The Bridge;* that of Uhland is observable in *Nuremberg.*

The Psalm of Life has been dissected line by line to prove how extensively its author plagiarized. Coleridge was another famous borrower. Assimilation, doubtless, had been so perfect in the case of each of these poets that they were unable to discriminate between what was acquired or original. Perhaps Mr. M. W. Hazeltine's statement on this subject affords a sufficient answer to the charge. Mr. Hazeltine says, "The simple test of an author's right to borrow is this: 'Is he able to lend?'"

The Building of the Ship is an instance of Longfellow's poetical acquisitiveness. One wonders, if he had not read Schiller, whether he could have written this fine poem, now reflective, again descriptive, and replete with sentiment. *The Wreck of the Hesperus* recalls the stern coast of Gloucester, the life of that seaport, and also at once swings us back to England's fifteenth and sixteenth century ballads. The song of three stanzas, " *Stay, stay at home, my heart, and rest,*" suggests in the metre, and some influence which it breathes, Tennyson's *The Princess.*

The three series of narrative poems called *Tales of a Wayside Inn*, the plan of which is undoubtedly based on *The Canterbury Tales,* shows an affluence of learning not necessarily profound. The descriptions of the Sicilian, the musician and the violin, are musical and happy. The student's tale of *The Falcon of Ser Federigo* is, as the poet says, taken from the *Decameron.* While it has Boccaccio's touch of utter simplicity, elegance, and pathos, it is obviously imperfect in the sequence of the descriptive passages.

The Legend of Rabbi Ben Levi, one of the tales of the Spanish Jew, is sometimes instanced as a proof of Longfellow's claim to the loftiest rank among poets. The interlude following *The Legend of Rabbi Ben Levi* is exquisite, and most gracefully introduces *King Robert of Sicily.* In *King Robert of Sicily* the story runs consistently and directly to its close. But this artistic poem, while not more artistic than Tennyson's *The Holy Grail,* cannot, however, compare with *The Holy Grail* in depth of spiritual suggestion.

Of all the poems in *Tales of a Wayside Inn,* none can be more pleasing to native ears and sentiment, and none quite so indicative of Longfellow's skill, because the themes had not been wrought over and upon by poets for centuries, as the landlord's tale, *Paul Revere's Ride,* the poet's tale, *The Birds of Killingworth,* and also his second one, *Lady Wentworth,* and, finally, the theologian's tale, *Elizabeth.*

As a sonneteer, Longfellow was very successful. In sonnets, his perception of the music in language, and his "gift of tongues," found adequate expression. As indicative of the ease with which his thought may be followed in this complex metrical handling, and because of a classic chasteness of description imbued with feeling and reflection, *The Old Bridge at Florence* and *Three Friends of Mine* are worthy of study, and may compare with some of Wordsworth's. While not possessing the ruggedness or the sculpturesque effect of those of Shakespeare, the Longfellow sonnets show the limpid clearness of their transalpine prototype.

The poems on which the poet's reputation mainly rests are *Evangeline* and *Hiawatha*.

To realize the beauty of its hexameter, *Evangeline* should be approached by reading, first, the translation, in hexameter, of Bishop Tegnér's *The Children of the Lord's Supper;* next, *Elizabeth;* and, third, *The Courtship of Miles Standish.*

Mr. M. W. Hazeltine complains that "the sluggish and ponderous effect produced by the use of the spondee in the fifth place is twenty times more frequent in *Evangeline* than in Ovid or Virgil;" but he also says, "*Evangeline* may well be ranked among the superlative exhibitions of pathetic power."

England has an abstract expression, and a greater one, of Puritan religious feeling in *Paradise Lost;* America has a concrete one, very sweet and human, although sincere and profound, not only in the moral attitude of Priscilla and Elizabeth, but in that also of the Catholic maiden, Evangeline.

Hiawatha has been called "the great opportunity of Longfellow's life."

The metre is a Finnish one, and was employed in the ancient Sagas, or epic poems, of the Scandinavians. It was unknown to English verse, except in translations, when *Hia-watha* was written.

To enjoy this folk-song, one must have an imagination kindred to that of Hans Christian Andersen, or of La Motte Fouqué. It should be read aloud, and with the abandon, if possible, of the improvisator.

It is full of Indian legends, and not of bizarre tales invented by Longfellow, as some adverse critics have asserted.

Hiawatha was the founder of Iroquois civilization, and revered as a god by those tribes. The poem is the story of his conquests over his enemies, the history of his friends, and also of other great Indian lights. It is an enchanting account of his courtship and marriage, of the troubles which overtook his people, the Ojibways, of the loss of his wife, Minnehaha, of the destruction of the mischievous Paupuk-keewis, and of Hiawatha's own translation to the Land of the Hereafter. Various Indian myths also are introduced, and the reader is startled by the appearance in legends of the North American Indians of the stories of Buddha and Achilles and the doctrines of altruism and the resurrection. To the editor's mind, *Hiawatha* is the most original contribution yet made in poetry to American literature.

Although the *Christus* was a work upon which endless time, labor, thought, and love were expended, it lacks unity, while containing many passages of superlative beauty.

The Spanish Gypsy seems like a crystallized, youthful product, and reminds the reader of the poet's almost juvenile handling of themes in *Outre-Mer*. It totally lacks dramatic power.

Michael Angelo, Longfellow's long, unfinished composition, is, in a certain coolness and severity of treatment, statuesque. It is as though the great architect and sculptor had cast the

glamour of his genius over the poem, which is seldom suffi-
ciently pictorial. Michael Angelo and Vittoria Colonna are
almost epic characters; and this Longfellow seems fully to
have realized in his patient and continued effort to ennoble
his drama. Nearly all of his work is too suggestive of other
poets; and *Michael Angelo*, as a highly original creation, is
condemned, when subjected to this crucial test. The dramatic form, together with the pose and conversation of the
various characters, insinuates into the critic's thought Goethe's
Torquato Tasso. There are passages so exquisitely beautiful
on Petrarch, that English, under the American poet's plastic
manipulation, breathes the melody and pathos combined which
immortalized the Italian singer. Again, Dante's fire, imagery,
and grandeur appear; but they are reflected, one feels, by
reason of Longfellow's universal sympathy. Presently and
suddenly the reader finds the style changing, as the burning
splendor of the setting sun lighting up a row of windows
will die away, leaving behind nothing but a cold, glittering,
and polished surface. There is, notwithstanding, in the
Michael Angelo, an evenly sustained treatment which makes
the drama superior to any comparison with that of *The Spanish
Gypsy.*

The poet's college lectures on Dante, and years of study
of that poet, led to his successful translation of the *Divine
Comedy.* The translation is an achievement in being nearly
literal, and still very musical. This work of his ripe maturity
is companioned by two of the finest things he ever wrote,
Kéramos and *Morituri Salutamus* — shining evidences of the
intellectual vitality often peculiar to the man or woman of
letters of advanced years.

Longfellow was highly esteemed abroad. A Swedish professor devoted the lectures on literature for an entire year to

the poet and his writings. He has been translated into all European languages.

He was the recipient of many literary honors. His own college made him LL.D. at twenty-one years of age. Harvard gave him the same degree at fifty-two. Cambridge honored him in this way when he was sixty-one years old, and Oxford made him D.C.L. when he was sixty-two. He was elected member of the Russian Academy of Science at sixty-six years of age, and of the Spanish Academy at seventy.

His last prose work, *Kavanagh*, was written in 1849. The characters are refined and suggestive. The story is discursive and sketchy; the style is fine.

After the age of forty-seven, Longfellow's literary effort was altogether in poetry. It is to be observed that, with the exception of *Evangeline*, which was published in 1847, most of his best poetry dates from the resignation of the Harvard professorship. *Hiawatha* was published in 1855. *The Courtship of Miles Standish* appeared in 1858; included in the volume was the first series of *Birds of Passage*. In 1863 *Tales of a Wayside Inn* and the second series of *Birds of Passage* were published. The completed translation of Dante was given to the public in 1867. *Christus: A Mystery* appeared in final form in 1873; to this year also belong *The Hanging of the Crane* and the last narratives of Part Third of *Tales of a Wayside Inn*. *Morituri Salutamus* was written in 1874, and portions of "Flight the Fifth" of *Birds of Passage* in 1878.

The poet was twice married. His first wife was Mary Storer Potter of Portland, Me. She died at Rotterdam, November, 1835. His second wife was Frances Elizabeth Appleton of Boston, Mass. She died in July, 1861. Through this second marriage Longfellow became owner of the celebrated Craigie House, which Washington made his headquarters on assuming command of the American army in 1876. Here the poet lived from 1837 till his death on March 24, 1882. The even tenor of his life was varied by a third journey to Europe in 1842, and a fourth and last journey in 1868.

Mr. Thomas Davidson truly says that " Longfellow's external life presents little that is of striking interest. It is the life of a modest, deep-hearted gentleman, whose highest ambition was to be a perfect man, and, through sympathy and love, to help others be the same. . . . In Longfellow . . . the poet was the flower and fruit of the man. His nature was essentially poetic, and his life incomparably the greatest of his poems."

EVANGELINE.

THIS is the forest primeval. The murmuring pines
and the hemlocks,
Bearded with moss, and in garments green, indistinct
in the twilight,
Stand like Druids of eld, with voices sad and prophetic,
Stand like harpers hoar, with beards that rest on their
bosoms.
Loud from its rocky caverns, the deep-voiced neighboring ocean   5
Speaks, and in accents disconsolate answers the wail
of the forest.

This is the forest primeval; but where are the hearts
that beneath it
Leaped like the roe, when he hears in the woodland the
voice of the huntsman ?
Where is the thatched-roofed village, the home of Acadian farmers, —
Men whose lives glided on like rivers that water the
woodlands,   10
Darkened by shadows of earth, but reflecting an image
of heaven ?

Waste are those pleasant farms, and the farmers for-
    ever departed !
Scattered like dust and leaves, when the mighty blasts
    of October
Seize them, and whirl them aloft, and sprinkle them
    far o'er the ocean.
Naught but tradition remains of the beautiful village of
    Grand-Pré.   15

Ye who believe in affection that hopes, and endures,
    and is patient,
Ye who believe in the beauty and strength of woman's
    devotion,
List to the mournful tradition, still sung by the pines
    of the forest;
List to a Tale of Love in Acadie, home of the happy.

PART THE FIRST.

I.

IN the Acadian land, on the shores of the Basin of
Minas,
Distant, secluded, still, the little village of Grand-Pré
Lay in the fruitful valley. Vast meadows stretched
to the eastward,
Giving the village its name, and pasture to flocks with-
out number.
Dikes, that the hands of the farmers had raised with
labor incessant,   5
Shut out the turbulent tides; but at stated seasons the
flood-gates
Opened, and welcomed the sea to wander at will o'er
the meadows.
West and south there were fields of flax, and orchards
and cornfields
Spreading afar and unfenced o'er the plain; and away
to the northward
Blomidon rose, and the forests old, and aloft on the
mountains   10
Sea-fogs pitched their tents, and mists from the mighty
Atlantic
Looked on the happy valley, but ne'er from their sta-
tion descended.

There, in the midst of its farms, reposed the Acadian
    village.
Strongly built were the houses, with frames of oak and
    of hemlock,
Such as the peasants of Normandy built in the reign
    of the Henries.   15
Thatched were the roofs, with dormer-windows; and
    gables projecting
Over the basement below protected and shaded the
    doorway.
There in the tranquil evenings of summer, when brightly
    the sunset
Lighted the village street, and gilded the vanes on the
    chimneys,
Matrons and maidens sat in snow-white caps and in
    kirtles   20
Scarlet and blue and green, with distaffs spinning the
    golden
Flax for the gossiping looms, whose noisy shuttles
    within doors
Mingled their sounds with the whirl of the wheels and
    the songs of the maidens.
Solemnly down the street came the parish priest, and
    the children
Paused in their play to kiss the hand he extended to
    bless them.   25
Reverend walked he among them; and up rose matrons
    and maidens,
Hailing his slow approach with words of affectionate
    welcome.

Then came the laborers home from the field, and serenely the sun sank
Down to his rest, and twilight prevailed. Anon from
the belfry
Softly the Angelus sounded, and over the roofs of the
village   30
Columns of pale blue smoke, like clouds of incense
ascending,
Rose from a hundred hearths, the homes of peace and
contentment.
Thus dwelt together in love these simple Acadian
farmers, —
Dwelt in the love of God and of man. Alike were
they free from
Fear, that reigns with the tyrant, and envy, the vice of
republics.   35
Neither locks had they to their doors, nor bars to their
windows ;
But their dwellings were open as day and the hearts
of the owners ;
There the richest was poor, and the poorest lived in
abundance.

Somewhat apart from the village, and nearer the
Basin of Minas,
Benedict Bellefontaine, the wealthiest farmer of Grand-
Pré,   40
Dwelt on his goodly acres ; and with him, directing his
household,

Gentle Evangeline lived, his child, and the pride of the
village.
Stalworth and stately in form was the man of seventy
winters;
Hearty and hale was he, an oak that is covered with
snow-flakes;
White as the snow were his locks, and his cheeks as
brown as the oak-leaves. 45
Fair was she to behold, that maiden of seventeen
summers.
Black were her eyes as the berry that grows on the
thorn by the wayside,
Black, yet how softly they gleamed beneath the brown
shades of her tresses!
Sweet was her breath as the breath of kine that feed
in the meadows.
When in the harvest heat she bore to the reapers at
noontide 50
Flagons of home-brewed ale, ah! fair in sooth was the
maiden.
Fairer was she when, on Sunday morn, while the bell
from its turret
Sprinkled with holy sounds the air, as the priest with
his hyssop
Sprinkles the congregation, and scatters blessings upon
them,
Down the long street she passed, with her chaplet of
beads and her missal, 55
Wearing her Norman cap, and her kirtle of blue, and
the ear-rings,

Brought in the olden time from France, and since, as
   an heirloom,
Handed down from mother to child, through long gen-
   erations.
But a celestial brightness — a more ethereal beauty —
Shone on her face and encircled her form, when, after
   confession,   60
Homeward serenely she walked with God's benediction
   upon her.
When she had passed, it seemed like the ceasing of
   exquisite music.

Firmly builded with rafters of oak, the house of the
   farmer
Stood on the side of a hill commanding the sea; and a
   shady
Sycamore grew by the door, with a woodbine wreathing
   around it.   65
Rudely carved was the porch, with seats beneath; and
   a footpath
Led through an orchard wide, and disappeared in the
   meadow.
Under the sycamore-tree were hives overhung by a
   penthouse,
Such as the traveller sees in regions remote by the road-
   side,
Built o'er a box for the poor, or the blessed image of
   Mary.   70
Farther down, on the slope of the hill, was the well
   with its moss-grown

Bucket, fastened with iron, and near it a trough for the
  horses.
Shielding the house from storms, on the north, were
  the barns and the farm-yard.
There stood the broad-wheeled wains and the antique
  ploughs and the harrows;
There were the folds for the sheep; and there, in his
  feathered seraglio,   75
Strutted the lordly turkey, and crowed the cock, with
  the selfsame
Voice that in ages of old had startled the penitent
  Peter.
Bursting with hay were the barns, themselves a village.
  In each one
Far o'er the gable projected a roof of thatch; and a
  staircase,
Under the sheltering eaves, led up to the odorous corn-
  loft.   80
There too the dove-cot stood, with its meek and inno-
  cent inmates
Murmuring ever of love; while above in the variant
  breezes
Numberless noisy weathercocks rattled and sang of
  mutation.

  Thus, at peace with God and the world, the farmer
    of Grand-Pré
Lived on his sunny farm, and Evangeline governed his
  household.   85

Many a youth, as he knelt in church and opened his
missal,
Fixed his eyes upon her as the saint of his deepest
devotion ;
Happy was he who might touch her hand or the hem
of her garment!
Many a suitor came to her door, by the darkness be-
friended,
And, ·as he knocked and waited to hear the sound of
her footsteps,   90
Knew not which beat the louder, his heart or the
knocker of iron ;
Or at the joyous feast of the Patron Saint of the
village,
Bolder grew, and pressed her hand in the dance as he
whispered
Hurried words · of love, that seemed a part of the
music.
But, among all who came, young Gabriel only was
welcome ;   95
Gabriel Lajeunesse, the son of Basil the blacksmith,
Who was a mighty man in the village, and honored
of all men ;
For, since the birth of time, throughout all ages and
nations,
Has the craft of the smith been held in repute by the
people.
Basil was Benedict's friend.   Their children from
earliest childhood   100

Grew up together as brother and sister; and Father
  Felician,
Priest and pedagogue both in the village, had taught
  them their letters
Out of the selfsame book, with the hymns of the church
  and the plain-song.
But when the hymn was sung, and the daily lesson
  completed,
Swiftly they hurried away to the forge of Basil the
  blacksmith.   105
There at the door they stood, with wondering eyes to
  behold him
Take in his leathern lap the hoof of the horse as a
  plaything,
Nailing the shoe in its place; while near him the tire
  of the cart-wheel
Lay like a fiery snake, coiled round in a circle of
  cinders.
Oft on autumnal eves, when without in the gathering
  darkness   110
Bursting with light seemed the smithy, through every
  cranny and crevice,
Warm by the forge within they watched the laboring
  bellows,
And as its panting ceased, and the sparks expired in
  the ashes,
Merrily laughed, and said they were nuns going into
  the chapel.
Oft on sledges in winter, as swift as the swoop of the
  eagle,   115

Down the hillside bounding, they glided away o'er the
  meadow.
Oft in the barns they climbed to the populous nests
  on the rafters,
Seeking with eager eyes that wondrous stone, which the
  swallow
Brings from the shore of the sea to restore the sight
  of its fledglings;
Lucky was he who found that stone in the nest of
  the swallow!   120
Thus passed a few swift years, and they no longer were
  children.
He was a valiant youth, and his face, like the face
  of the morning,
Gladdened the earth with its light, and ripened thought
  into action.
She was a woman now, with the heart and hopes of a
  woman.
" Sunshine of Saint Eulalie " was she called; for that
  was the sunshine   125
Which, as the farmers believed, would load their orchards with apples;
She, too, would bring to her husband's house delight
  and abundance,
Filling it with love and the ruddy faces of children.

II.

Now had the season returned, when the nights grow
  colder and longer
And the retreating sun the sign of the Scorpion en-
  ters.   130
Birds of passage sailed through the leaden air, from the
  ice-bound,
Desolate northern bays to the shores of tropical islands.
Harvests were gathered in ; and wild with the winds of
  September
Wrestled the trees of the forest, as Jacob of old with
  the angel.
All the signs foretold a winter long and inclement.   135
Bees, with prophetic instinct of want, had hoarded their
  honey
Till the hives overflowed ; and the Indian hunters as-
  serted
Cold would the winter be, for thick was the fur of the
  foxes.
Such was the advent of autumn.   Then followed that
  beautiful season,
Called by the pious Acadian peasants the Summer of
  All-Saints !   140
Filled was the air with a dreamy and magical light ;
  and the landscape
Lay as if new-created in all the freshness of childhood.
Peace seemed to reign upon earth, and the restless heart
  of the ocean

Was for a moment consoled. All sounds were in harmony blended.
Voices of children at play, the crowing of cocks in the
farm-yards, 145
Whir of wings in the drowsy air, and the cooing of
pigeons,
All were subdued and low as the murmurs of love, and
the great sun
Looked with the eye of love through the golden vapors
around him;
While arrayed in its robes of russet and scarlet and
yellow,
Bright with the sheen of the dew, each glittering tree
of the forest 150
Flashed like the plane-tree the Persian adorned with
mantles and jewels.

Now recommenced the reign of rest and affection
and stillness.
Day with its burden and heat had departed, and twilight descending
Brought back the evening star to the sky, and the herds
to the homestead.
Pawing the ground they came, and resting their necks
on each other, 155
And with their nostrils distended inhaling the freshness
of evening.
Foremost, bearing the bell, Evangeline's beautiful
heifer,

Proud of her snow-white hide, and the ribbon that
waved from her collar,
Quietly paced and slow, as if conscious of human
affection.
Then came the shepherd back with his bleating flocks
from the seaside,   160
Where was their favorite pasture.   Behind them followed the watch-dog, .
Patient, full of importance, and grand in the pride of
his instinct,
Walking from side to side with a lordly air, and
superbly
Waving his bushy tail, and urging forward the strag-
glers;
Regent of flocks was he when the shepherd slept; their
protector,   165
When from the forest at night, through the starry
silence the wolves howled.
Late, with the rising moon, returned the wains from
the marshes,
Laden with briny hay, that filled the air with its odor.
Cheerily neighed the steeds, with dew on their manes
and their fetlocks,
While aloft on their shoulders the wooden and pon-
derous saddles,   170
Painted with brilliant dyes, and adorned with tassels
of crimson,
Nodded in bright array, like hollyhocks heavy with
blossoms.

Patiently stood the cows meanwhile, and yielded their
    udders
Unto the milkmaid's hand; whilst loud and in regular
    cadence
Into the sounding pails the foaming streamlets de-
    scended.   175
Lowing of cattle and peals of laughter were heard in
    the farm-yard,
Echoed back by the barns. Anon they sank into still-
    ness;
Heavily closed, with a jarring sound, the valves of the
    barn-doors,
Rattled the wooden bars, and all for a season was
    silent.

In-doors, warm by the wide-mouthed fireplace, idly
    the farmer   180
Sat in his elbow-chair and watched how the flames
    and the smoke-wreaths
Struggled together like foes in a burning city. Behind
    him,
Nodding and mocking along the wall, with gestures
    fantastic,
Darted his own huge shadow, and vanished away into
    darkness.
Faces, clumsily carved in oak, on the back of his
    arm-chair   185
Laughed in the flickering light; and the pewter plates
    on the dresser

Caught and reflected the flame, as shields of armies
the sunshine.
Fragments of song the old man sang, and carols of
Christmas,
Such as at home, in the olden time, his fathers before
him
Sang in their Norman orchards and bright Burgun-
dian vineyards.   190
Close at her father's side was the gentle Evangeline
seated,
Spinning flax for the loom, that stood in the corner
behind her.
Silent awhile were its treadles, at rest was its diligent
shuttle,
While the monotonous drone of the wheel, like the
drone of a bagpipe,
Followed the old man's song and united the fragments
together.   195
As in a church, when the chant of the choir at intervals
ceases,
Footfalls are heard in the aisles, or words of the priest
at the altar,
So, in each pause of the song, with measured motion the
clock clicked.

Thus as they sat, there were footsteps heard, and,
suddenly lifted,
Sounded the wooden latch, and the door swung back
on its hinges.   200

Benedict knew by the hob-nailed shoes it was Basil the
blacksmith,
And by her beating heart Evangeline knew who was
with him.
" Welcome ! " the farmer exclaimed, as their footsteps
paused on the threshold,
"Welcome, Basil, my friend !   Come, take thy place
on the settle
Close by the chimney-side, which is always empty with-
out thee ;   205
Take from the shelf overhead thy pipe and the box of
tobacco ;
Never so much thyself art thou as when through the
curling
Smoke of the pipe or the forge thy friendly and jovial
face gleams
Round and red as the harvest moon through the mist
of the marshes."
Then, with a smile of content, thus answered Basil the
blacksmith,   210
Taking with easy air the accustomed seat by the fire-
side : —
" Benedict Bellefontaine, thou hast ever thy jest and
thy ballad !   .
Ever in cheerfullest mood art thou, when others are
filled with
Gloomy forebodings of ill, and see only ruin before
them.
Happy art thou, as if every day thou hadst picked up
a horseshoe."   215

Pausing a moment, to take the pipe that Evangeline
    brought him,
And with a coal from the embers had lighted, he slowly
    continued : —
  "Four days now are passed since the English ships
    at their anchors
Ride in the Gaspereau's mouth, with their cannon
    pointed against us.
What their design may be is unknown; but all are
    commanded   220
On the morrow to meet in the church, where his Maj-
    esty's mandate
Will be proclaimed as law in the land.   Alas! in the
    meantime
Many surmises of evil alarm the hearts of the peo-
    ple."
Then made answer the farmer : "Perhaps some friend-
    lier purpose
Brings these ships to our shores.   Perhaps the harvests
    in England   225
By untimely rains or untimelier heat have been blighted,
And from our bursting barns they would feed their
    cattle and children."
  "Not so thinketh the folk in the village," said
    warmly, the blacksmith,
Shaking his head, as in doubt; then, heaving a sigh,
    he continued : —
  "Louisburg is not forgotten, nor Beau Séjour, nor
    Port Royal.   230

Many already have fled to the forest, and lurk on its
    outskirts,
Waiting with anxious hearts the dubious fate of to-
    morrow.
Arms have been taken from us, and warlike weapons
    of all kinds;
Nothing is left but the blacksmith's sledge and the
    scythe of the mower."
Then with a pleasant smile made answer the jovial
    farmer : —   235
  "Safer are we unarmed, in the midst of our flocks
    and our cornfields,
Safer within these peaceful dikes, besieged by the
    ocean,
Than our fathers in forts, besieged by the enemy's
    cannon.
Fear no evil, my friend, and to-night may no shadow
    of sorrow
Fall on this house and hearth; for this is the night
    of the contract.   240
Built are the house and the barn. The merry lads
    of the village
Strongly have built them and well; and, breaking
    the glebe round about them,
Filled the barn with hay, and the house with food
    for a twelvemonth.
René Leblanc will be here anon, with his papers and
    inkhorn.
Shall we not then be glad, and rejoice in the joy of
    our children ? "   245

As apart by the window she stood, with her hand in
  her lover's,
Blushing Evangeline heard the words that her father
  had spoken,
And as they died on his lips, the worthy notary
  entered.

III.

BENT like a laboring oar, that toils in the surf of
  the ocean,
Bent, but not broken, by age was the form of the
  notary public;   250
Shocks of yellow hair, like the silken floss of the maize,
  hung
Over his shoulders; his forehead was high; and glasses
  with horn bows
Sat astride on his nose, with a look of wisdom supernal.
Father of twenty children was he, and more than a
  hundred
Children's children rode on his knee, and heard his
  great watch tick.   255
Four long years in the times of the war had he languished a captive,
Suffering much in an old French fort as the friend
  of the English.
Now, though warier grown, without all guile or suspicion,
Ripe in wisdom was he, but patient, and simple, and
  childlike.

He was beloved by all, and most of all by the chil-
dren;   260
For he told them tales of the Loup-garou in the forest,
And of the goblin that came in the night to water the
horses,
And of the white Létiche, the ghost of a child who
unchristened
Died, and was doomed to haunt unseen the chambers
of children;
And how on Christmas eve the oxen talked in the
stable,   265
And how the fever was cured by a spider shut up in
a nutshell,
And of the marvellous powers of four-leaved clover
and horseshoes,
With whatsoever else was writ in the lore of the village.
Then up rose from his seat by the fireside Basil the
blacksmith,
Knocked from his pipe the ashes, and slowly extending
his right hand,   270
"Father Leblanc," he exclaimed, "thou hast heard
the talk in the village,
And, perchance, canst tell us some news of these ships
and their errand."
Then with modest demeanor made answer the notary
public, —
"Gossip enough have I heard, in sooth, yet am never
the wiser;

Yet am I not of those who imagine some evil intention
Brings them here, for we are at peace; and why then
    molest us ? "
  " God's name ! " shouted the hasty and somewhat
    irascible blacksmith;
  " Must we in all things look for the how, and the
    why, and the wherefore ?
Daily injustice is done, and might is the right of the
    strongest ! "
But without heeding his warmth, continued the notary
    public, —   280
  " Man is unjust, but God is just; and finally justice
Triumphs; and well I remember a story, that often
    consoled me,
When as a captive I lay in the old French fort at Port
    Royal."
This was the old man's favorite tale, and he loved to
    repeat it
When his neighbors complained that any injustice was
    done them.   285
  " Once in an ancient city, whose name I no longer
    remember,
Raised aloft on a column, a brazen statue of Justice
Stood in the public square, upholding the scales in its
    left hand,
And in its right a sword, as an emblem that justice
    presided
Over the laws of the land, and the hearts and homes
    of the people.   290

Even the birds had built their nests in the scales of
   the balance,
Having no fear of the sword that flashed in the sunshine above them.
But in the course of time the laws of the land were
   corrupted ;
Might took the place of right, and the weak were
   oppressed, and the mighty
Ruled with an iron rod. Then it chanced in a noble-
   man's palace   295
That a necklace of pearls was lost, and erelong a
   suspicion
Fell on an orphan girl who lived as a maid in the
   household.
She, after form of trial condemned to die on the scaf-
   fold,
Patiently met her doom at the foot of the statue of
   Justice.
As to her Father in heaven her innocent spirit as-
   cended,   300
Lo ! o'er the city a tempest rose ; and the bolts of the
   thunder
Smote the statue of bronze, and hurled in wrath from
   its left hand
Down on the pavement below the clattering scales of
   the balance,
And in the hollow thereof was found the nest of a
   magpie,
Into whose clay-built walls the necklace of pearls was
   inwoven."   305

Silenced, but not convinced, when the story was ended, the blacksmith
Stood like a man who fain would speak, but findeth no language ;
All his thoughts were congealed into lines on his face, as the vapors
Freeze in fantastic shapes on the window-frames in the winter.

Then Evangeline lighted the brazen lamp on the table,   310
Filled, till it overflowed, the pewter tankard with home-brewed
Nut-brown ale, that was famed for its strength in the village of Grand-Pré ;
While from his pocket the notary drew his papers and inkhorn,
Wrote with a steady hand the date and the age of the parties,
Naming the dower of the bride in flocks of sheep and in cattle.   315
Orderly all things proceeded, and duly and well were completed,
And the great seal of the law was set like a sun on the margin.
Then from his leathern pouch the farmer threw on the table
Three times the old man's fee in solid pieces of silver ;

And the notary rising, and blessing the bride and the
  bridegroom, 320
Lifted aloft the tankard of ale and drank to their
  welfare.
Wiping the foam from his lip, he solemnly bowed and
  departed,
While in silence the others sat and mused by the fire-
  side,
Till Evangeline brought the draught-board out of its
  corner.
Soon was the game begun. In friendly contention the
  old men 325
Laughed at each lucky hit, or unsuccessful manœuvre,
Laughed when a man was crowned, or a breach was
  made in the king-row.
Meanwhile apart, in the twilight gloom of a window's
  embrasure,
Sat the lovers, and whispered together, _beholding the
  moon rise
Over the pallid sea, and the silvery mists of the
  meadows. 330
Silently one by one, in the infinite meadows of heaven,
Blossomed the lovely stars, the forget-me-nots of the
  angels.

Thus was the evening passed. Anon the bell from
  the belfry
Rang out the hour of nine, the village curfew, and
  straightway

Rose the guests and departed; and silence reigned in
    the household.   335
Many a farewell word and sweet good-night on the door-
    step
Lingered long in Evangeline's heart, and filled it with
    gladness.
Carefully then were covered the embers that glowed on
    the hearth-stone,
And on the oaken stairs resounded the tread of the
    farmer.
Soon with a soundless step the foot of Evangeline
    followed.   340
Up the staircase moved a luminous space in the darkness,
Lighted less by the lamp than the shining face of the
    maiden.
Silent she passed the hall, and entered the door of
    her chamber.
Simple that chamber was, with its curtains of white,
    and its clothes-press
Ample and high, on whose spacious shelves were care-
    fully folded   345
Linen and woollen stuffs, by the hand of Evangeline
    woven.
This was the precious dower she would bring to her
    husband in marriage,
Better than flocks and herds, being proofs of her skill
    as a housewife.
Soon she extinguished her lamp, for the mellow and
    radiant moonlight

Streamed through the windows, and lighted the room,
till the heart of the maiden   350
Swelled and obeyed its power, like the tremulous tides
of the ocean.
Ah! she was fair, exceeding fair to behold, as she
stood with
Naked snow-white feet on the gleaming floor of. her
chamber!
Little she dreamed that below, among the trees of the
orchard,
Waited her lover and watched for the gleam of her
lamp and her shadow.   355
Yet were her thoughts of him, and at times a feeling
of sadness
Passed o'er her soul, as the sailing shade of clouds in
the moonlight
Flitted across the floor and darkened the room for a
moment.
And, as she gazed from the window, she saw serenely
the moon pass
Forth from the folds of a cloud, and one star follow
her footsteps,   360
As out of Abraham's tent young Ishmael wandered with
Hagar!

IV.

PLEASANTLY rose next morn the sun on the village of
Grand-Pré.
Pleasantly gleamed in the soft, sweet air the Basin of
Minas,

Where the ships, with their wavering shadows, were
    riding at anchor.
Life had long been astir in the village, and clamorous
    labor   365
Knocked with its hundred hands at the golden gates
    of the morning.
Now from the country around, from the farms and
    neighboring hamlets,
Came in their holiday dresses the blithe Acadian
    peasants.
Many a glad good-morrow and jocund laugh from the
    young folk
Made the bright air brighter, as up from the numerous
    meadows,   370
Where no path could be seen but the track of wheels
    in the greensward,
Group after group appeared, and joined, or passed on
    the highway.
Long ere noon, in the village all sounds of labor were
    silenced.
Thronged were the streets with people; and noisy
    groups at the house-doors
Sat in the cheerful sun, and rejoiced and gossiped
    together.   375
Every house was an inn, where all were welcomed and
    feasted;
For with this simple people, who lived like brothers
    together,
All things were held in common, and what one had was
    another's.

Yet under Benedict's roof hospitality seemed more
  abundant:
For Evangeline stood among the guests of her father;
Bright was her face with smiles, and words of welcome
  and gladness
Fell from her beautiful lips, and blessed the cup as she
  gave it.

Under the open sky, in the odorous air of the
  orchard,
Stript of its golden fruit, was spread the feast of
  betrothal.
There in the shade of the porch were the priest and
  the notary seated;   385
There good Benedict sat, and sturdy Basil the black-
  smith.
Not far withdrawn from these, by the cider-press and
  the beehives,
Michael the fiddler was placed, with the gayest of
  hearts and of waistcoats.
Shadow and light from the leaves alternately played
  on his snow-white
Hair, as it waved in the wind; and the jolly face of
  the fiddler   390
Glowed like a living coal when the ashes are blown
  from the embers.
Gayly the old man sang to the vibrant sound of his fiddle,
Tous les Bourgeois de Chartres, and *Le Carillon de
  Dunquerque*,

And anon with his wooden shoes beat time to the
music.
Merrily, merrily whirled the wheels of the dizzying
dances   395
Under the orchard trees and down the path to the
meadows;
Old folk and young together, and children mingled
among them.
Fairest of all the maids was Evangeline, Benedict's
daughter!
Noblest of all the youths was Gabriel, son of the
blacksmith!

So passed the morning away.   And lo! with a
summons sonorous   400
Sounded the bell from its tower, and over the meadows
a drum beat.
Thronged erelong was the church with men.   Without,
in the churchyard,
Waited the women.   They stood by the graves, and
hung on the headstones
Garlands of autumn-leaves and evergreens fresh from
the forest.
Then came the guard from the ships, and marching
proudly among them   405
Entered the sacred portal.   With loud and dissonant
clangor
Echoed the sound of their brazen drums from ceiling
and casement, —

Echoed a moment only, and slowly the ponderous
portal
Closed, and in silence the crowd awaited the will of
the soldiers.
Then uprose their commander, and spake from the
steps of the altar,   410
Holding aloft in his hands, with its seals, the royal
commission.
"You are convened this day," he said, "by his
Majesty's orders.
Clement and kind has he been; but how you have
answered his kindness,
Let your own hearts reply! To my natural make
and my temper
Painful the task is I do, which to you I know must
be grievous.   415
Yet must I bow and obey, and deliver the will of
our monarch;
Namely, that all your lands, and dwellings, and cattle
of all kinds
Forfeited be to the crown; and that you yourselves
from this province
Be transported to other lands. God grant you may
dwell there
Ever as faithful subjects, a happy and peaceable people!
Prisoners now I declare you; for such is his Maj-
esty's pleasure!"
As, when the air is serene in sultry solstice of sum-
mer,

Suddenly gathers a storm, and the deadly sling of the
  hailstones
Beats down the farmer's corn in the field and shatters
  his windows,
Hiding the sun, and strewing the ground with thatch
  from the house-roofs,   425
Bellowing fly the herds, and seek to break their en-
  closures ;
So on the hearts of the people descended the words
  of the speaker.
Silent a moment they stood in speechless wonder, and
  then rose
Louder and ever louder a wail of sorrow and anger,
And, by one impulse moved, they madly rushed to
  the door-way.   430
Vain was the hope of escape; and cries and fierce
  imprecations
Rang through the house of prayer; and high o'er the
  heads of the others
Rose, with his arms uplifted, the figure of Basil the
  blacksmith,
As, on a stormy sea, a spar is tossed by the bil-
  lows.
Flushed was his face and distorted with passion; and
  wildly he shouted, —   435
  " Down with the tyrants of England !   We never
  have sworn them allegiance !
Death to these foreign soldiers, who seize on our
  homes and our harvests ! "

More he fain would have said, but the merciless hand
    of a soldier
Smote him upon the mouth, and dragged him down
    to the pavement.

  In the midst of the strife and tumult of angry
    contention,   440
Lo! the door of the chancel opened, and Father
    Felician
Entered with serious mien, and ascended the steps of
    the altar.
Raising his reverend hand, with a gesture he awed
    into silence
All that clamorous throng; and thus he spake to his
    people ;
Deep were his tones and solemn; in accents measured
    and mournful   445
Spake he, as, after the tocsin's alarum, distinctly the
    clock strikes.
  "What is this that ye do, my children? What
    madness has seized you ?
Forty years of my life have I labored among you,
    and taught you,
Not in word alone, but in deed, to love one an-
    other!
Is this the fruit of my toils, of my vigils and prayers
    and privations ?   450
Have you so soon forgotten all lessons of love and
    forgiveness ?

This is the house of the Prince of Peace, and would
    you profane it
Thus with violent deeds and hearts overflowing with
    hatred ?
Lo! where the crucified Christ from his cross is gazing
    upon you!
See! in those sorrowful eyes what meekness and holy
    compassion !   455
Hark! how those lips still repeat the prayer, ' O
    Father, forgive them !'
Let us repeat that prayer in the hour when the wicked
    assail us,
Let us repeat it now, and say, ' O Father, forgive
    them !' "
Few were his words of rebuke, but deep in the hearts
    of his people
Sank they, and sobs of contrition succeeded the passion-
    ate outbreak,   460
While they repeated his prayer, and said, "O Father,
    forgive them !"

Then came the evening service. The tapers gleamed
    from the altar.   •
Fervent and deep was the voice of the priest, and the
    people responded,
Not with their lips alone, but their hearts ; and the
    Ave Maria
Sang they, and fell on their knees, and their souls,
    with devotion translated,   465

Rose on the ardor of prayer, like Elijah ascending to
heaven.

Meanwhile had spread in the village the tidings of
ill, and on all sides
Wandered, wailing, from house to house the women
and children.
Long at her father's door Evangeline stood, with her
right hand
Shielding her eyes from the level rays of the sun that,
descending,   470
Lighted the village street with mysterious splendor,
and roofed each
Peasant's cottage with golden thatch, and emblazoned
its windows.
Long within had been spread the snow-white cloth on
the table;
There stood the wheaten loaf, and the honey fragrant
with wild-flowers;
There stood the tankard of ale, and the cheese fresh
from the dairy,   475
And, at the head of the board, the great arm-chair of
the farmer.   ·
Thus did Evangeline wait at her father's door, as the
sunset
Threw the long shadows of trees o'er the broad ambrosial meadows.
Ah! on her spirit within a deeper shadow had fallen,
And from the fields of her soul a fragrance celestial
ascended, —   480

Charity, meekness, love, and hope, and forgiveness, and
    patience!
Then, all-forgetful of self, she wandered into the
    village,
Cheering with looks and words the mournful hearts of
    women,
As o'er the darkening fields with lingering steps they
    departed,
Urged by their household cares, and the weary feet
    of their children.   485
Down sank the great red sun, and in golden, glimmer-
    ing vapors
Veiled the light of his face, like the Prophet descend-
    ing from Sinai.
Sweetly over the village the bell of the Angelus
    sounded.

Meanwhile, amid the gloom, by the church Evan-
    geline lingered.
All was silent within; and in vain at the door and
    the windows   .   490
Stood she, and listened and looked, till, overcome by
    emotion,
"Gabriel!" cried she aloud with tremulous voice;
    but no answer
Came from the graves of the dead, nor the gloomier
    grave of the living.
Slowly at length she returned to the tenantless house
    of her father.

Smouldered the fire on the hearth, on the board was
    the supper untasted,   495
Empty and drear was each room, and haunted with
    phantoms of terror.
Sadly echoed her step on the stair and the floor of
    her chamber.
In the dead of the night she heard the disconsolate
    rain fall
Loud on the withered leaves of the sycamore-tree by
    the window.
Keenly the lightning flashed; and the voice of the
    echoing thunder   500
Told her that God was in heaven, and governed the
    world he created!
Then she remembered the tale she had heard of the
    justice of Heaven;
Soothed was her troubled soul, and she peacefully
    slumbered till morning.

V.

FOUR times the sun had risen and set; and now on
    the fifth day
Cheerily called the cock to the sleeping maids of the
    farm-house.   505
Soon o'er the yellow fields, in silent and mournful
    procession,
Came from the neighboring hamlets and farms the
    Acadian women,

Driving in ponderous wains their household goods to
the sea-shore,
Pausing and looking back to gaze once more on their
dwellings,
Ere they were shut from sight by the winding road
and the woodland.   510
Close at their sides their children ran, and urged on
the oxen,
While in their little hands they clasped some fragments of playthings.

Thus to the Gaspereau's mouth they hurried; and
there on the sea-beach
Piled in confusion lay the household goods of the
peasants.
All day long between the shore and the ships did
the boats ply;   515
All day long the wains came laboring down from the
village.
Late in the afternoon, when the sun was near to his
setting,
Echoed far o'er the fields came the roll of drums from
the churchyard.
Thither the women and children thronged. On a sudden the church-doors
Opened, and forth came the guard, and marching in
gloomy procession   520
Followed the long-imprisoned, but patient, Acadian
farmers.

Even as pilgrims, who journey afar from their homes
and their country,
Sing as they go, and in singing forget they are weary
and wayworn,
So with songs on their lips the Acadian peasants de-
scended
Down from the church to the shore, amid their wives
and their daughters.   525
Foremost the young men came; and, raising together
their voices,
Sang with tremulous lips a chant of the Catholic
Missions : —
" Sacred heart of the Saviour ! O inexhaustible
fountain !
Fill our hearts this day with strength and submission
and patience ! "
Then the old men, as they marched, and the women
that stood by the wayside   530
Joined in the sacred psalm, and the birds in the
sunshine above them
Mingled their notes therewith, like voices of spirits
departed.

Half-way down to the shore Evangeline waited in
silence,
Not overcome with grief, but strong in the hour of
affliction, —
Calmly and sadly she waited, until the procession approached her,   535

And she beheld the face of Gabriel pale with emotion.
Tears then filled her eyes, and, eagerly running to meet
 him,
Clasped she his hands, and laid her head on his shoul-
 der, and whispered, —
 "Gabriel! be of good cheer! for if we love one
 another
Nothing, in truth, can harm us, whatever mischances
 may happen!"   540
Smiling she spake these words; then suddenly paused,
 for her father
Saw she slowly advancing. Alas! how changed was
 his aspect!
Gone was the glow from his cheek, and the fire from
 his eye, and his footstep
Heavier seemed with the weight of the heavy heart
 in his bosom.
But with a smile and a sigh, she clasped his neck
 and embraced him,   545
Speaking words of endearment where words of comfort
 availed not.
Thus to the Gaspereau's mouth moved on that mournful procession.

 There disorder prevailed, and the tumult and stir
 of embarking.
Busily plied the freighted boats; and in the confusion
Wives were torn from their husbands, and mothers,
 too late, saw their children   550

Left on the land, extending their arms, with wildest
    entreaties.
So unto separate ships were Basil and Gabriel car-
    ried,
While in despair on the shore Evangeline stood with
    her father.
Half the task was not done when the sun went down,
    and the twilight
Deepened and darkened around ; and in haste the ref-
    luent ocean   555
Fled away from the shore, and left the line of the
    sand-beach
Covered with waifs of the tide, with kelp and the
    slipping sea-weed.
Farther back in the midst of the household goods and
    the wagons,
Like to a gypsy camp, or a leaguer after a battle,
All escape cut off by the sea, and the sentinels near
    them,   560
Lay encamped for the night the houseless Acadian
    farmers.
Back to its nethermost caves retreated the bellowing
    ocean,
Dragging adown the beach the rattling pebbles, and
    leaving
Inland and far up the shore the stranded boats of the
    sailors.
Then, as the night descended, the herds returned from
    their pastures ;   565

Sweet was the moist still air with the odor of milk
    from their udders;
Lowing they waited, and long, at the well-known bars
    of the farm-yard, —
Waited and looked in vain for the voice and the hand
    of the milk-maid.
Silence reigned in the streets; from the church no An-
    gelus sounded,
Rose no smoke from the roofs, and gleamed no lights
    from the windows.   570

But on the shores meanwhile the evening fires had
    been kindled,
Built of the drift-wood thrown on the sands from
    wrecks in the tempest.
Round them shapes of gloom and sorrowful faces were
    gathered,
Voices of women were heard, and of men, and the cry-
    ing of children.
Onward from fire to fire, as from hearth to hearth in
    his parish,   575
Wandered the faithful priest, consoling and blessing
    and cheering,
Like unto shipwrecked Paul on Melita's desolate sea-
    shore.
Thus he approached the place where Evangeline sat
    with her father,
And in the flickering light beheld the face of the old
    man,

Haggard and hollow and wan, and without either
    thought or emotion,   580
E'en as the face of a clock from which the hands have
    been taken.
Vainly Evangeline strove with words and caresses to
    cheer him,
Vainly offered him food ; yet he moved not, he looked
    not, he spake not,
But, with a vacant stare, ever gazed at the flickering
    fire-light.
    " *Benedicite !* " murmured the priest, in tones of com-
    passion.   585
More he fain would have said, but his heart was full,
    and his accents
Faltered and paused on his lips, as the feet of a child
    on a threshold,
Hushed by the scene he beholds, and the awful pres-
    ence of sorrow.
Silently, therefore, he laid his hand on the head of the
    maiden,
Raising his tearful eyes to the silent stars that above
    them   590
Moved on their way, unperturbed by the wrongs and
    sorrows of mortals.
Then sat he down at her side, and they wept together
    in silence.

    Suddenly rose from the south a light, as in autumn
    the blood-red

Moon climbs the crystal walls of heaven, and o'er the
 horizon
Titan-like stretches its hundred hands upon the mountain and meadow,   595
Seizing the rocks and the rivers and piling huge shadows together.
Broader and ever broader it gleamed on the roofs of
 the village,
Gleamed on the sky and sea, and the ships that lay in
 the roadstead.
Columns of shining smoke uprose, and flashes of flame
 were
Thrust through their folds and withdrawn, like the
 quivering hands of a martyr.   600
Then as the wind seized the gleeds and the burning
 thatch, and, uplifting,
Whirled them aloft through the air, at once from a
 hundred house-tops
Started the sheeted smoke with flashes of flame intermingled.

These things beheld in dismay the crowd on the
 shore and on shipboard.
Speechless at first they stood, then cried aloud in their
 anguish,   602
 " We shall behold no more our homes in the village
 of Grand-Pré ! "
Loud on a sudden the cocks began to crow in the farm-
 yards,

Thinking the day had dawned; and anon the lowing
    of cattle
Came on the evening breeze, by the barking of dogs
    interrupted.
Then rose a sound of dread, such as startles the sleep-
    ing encampments   610
Far in the western prairies or forests that skirt the
    Nebraska,
When the wild horses affrighted sweep by with the
    speed of the whirlwind,
Or the loud bellowing herds of buffaloes rush to the
    river.
Such was the sound that arose on the night, as the
    herds and the horses
Broke through their folds and fences, and madly rushed
    o'er the meadows.   615

Overwhelmed with the sight, yet speechless, the
    priest and the maiden
Gazed on the scene of terror that reddened and widened
    before them;
And as they turned at length to speak to their silent
    companion,
Lo! from his seat he had fallen, and stretched abroad
    on the sea-shore
Motionless lay his form, from which the soul had
    departed.   620
Slowly the priest uplifted the lifeless head, and the
    maiden

Knelt at her father's side, and wailed aloud in her terror.
Then in a swoon she sank, and lay with her head on
 his bosom.
Through the long night she lay in deep, oblivious
 slumber;
And when she awoke from the trance, she beheld a
 multitude near her.   625
Faces of friends she beheld, that were mournfully
 gazing upon her,
Pallid, with tearful eyes, and looks of saddest compassion.
Still the blaze of the burning village illumined the
 landscape,
Reddened the sky overhead, and gleamed on the faces
 around her,
And like the day of doom it seemed to her wavering
 senses.   630
Then a familiar voice she heard, as it said to the
 people, —
"Let us bury him here by the sea. When a happier
 season
Brings us again to our homes from the unknown land
 of our exile,
Then shall his sacred dust be piously laid in the
 churchyard."
Such were the words of the priest. And there in
 haste by the sea-side,   635
Having the glare of the burning village for funeral
 torches,

But without bell or book, they buried the farmer of
  Grand-Pré.
And as the voice of the priest repeated the service
  of sorrow,
Lo! with a mournful sound, like the voice of a vast
  congregation,
Solemnly answered the sea, and mingled its roar with
  the dirges.   640
'Twas the returning tide, that afar from the waste of
  the ocean,
With the first dawn of the day, came heaving and
  hurrying landward.
Then recommenced once more the stir and noise of
  embarking;
And with the ebb of the tide the ships sailed out
  of the harbor,
Leaving behind them the dead on the shore, and the
  village in ruins.   645

PART THE SECOND.

I

MANY a weary year had passed since the burning of
Grand-Pré,
When on the falling tide the freighted vessels de-
parted,
Bearing a nation, with all its household gods, into exile,
Exile without an end, and without an example in story.
Far asunder, on separate coasts, the Acadians landed;
Scattered were they, like flakes of snow, when the
wind from the northeast   6
Strikes aslant through the fogs that darken the Banks
of Newfoundland.
Friendless, homeless, hopeless, they wandered from
city to city,
From the cold lakes of the North to sultry Southern
savannas, — .
From the bleak shores of the sea to the lands where
the Father of Waters   10
Seizes the hills in his hands, and drags them down
to the ocean,
Deep in their souls to bury the scattered bones of
the mammoth.
Friends they sought and homes; and many, despair-
ing, heart-broken,

Asked of the earth but a grave, and no longer a
    friend nor a fireside.
Written their history stands on tablets of stone in
    the churchyards.   15
Long among them was seen a maiden who waited and
    wandered,
Lowly and meek in spirit, and patiently suffering all
    things.
Fair was she and young : but, alas ! before her ex-
    tended,
Dreary and vast and silent, the desert of life, with
    its pathway
Marked by the graves of those who had sorrowed and
    suffered before her,   20
Passions long extinguished, and hopes long dead and
    abandoned,
As the emigrant's way o'er the Western desert is
    marked by
Camp-fires long consumed, and bones that bleach in
    the sunshine.
Something there was in her life incomplete, imper-
    fect, unfinished ;
As if a morning of June, with all its music and
    sunshine,   25
Suddenly paused in the sky, and, fading, slowly de-
    scended
Into the east again, from whence it late had arisen.
Sometimes she lingered in towns, till, urged by the
    fever within her,

Urged by a restless longing, the hunger and thirst
   of the spirit,
She would commence again her endless search and
   endeavor ;   30
Sometimes in churchyards strayed, and gazed on the
   crosses and tombstones,
Sat by some nameless grave, and thought that perhaps
   in its bosom
He was already at rest, and she longed to slumber be-
   side him.
Sometimes a rumor, a hearsay, an inarticulate whisper,
Came with its airy hand to point and beckon her for-
   ward.   35
Sometimes she spake with those who had seen her be-
   loved and known him,
But it was long ago, in some far-off place or forgotten.
   " Gabriel Lajeunesse ! " they said ; " Oh yes ! we
   have seen him.
He was with Basil the blacksmith, and both have gone
   to the prairies ;
Coureurs-des-Bois are they, and famous hunters and
   trappers."   40
   " Gabriel Lajeunesse ! " said others ; " Oh yes ! we
   have seen him.
He is a Voyageur in the lowlands of Louisiana."
Then would they say, " Dear child ! why dream and
   wait for him longer ?
Are there not other youths as fair as Gabriel ? others
Who have hearts as tender and true, and spirits as loyal ?

Here is Baptiste Leblanc, the notary's son, who has
   loved thee
Many a tedious year; come, give him· thy hand and
   be happy!
Thou art too fair to be left to braid St. Catherine's
   tresses."
Then would Evangeline answer, serenely but sadly, " I
   cannot!
Whither my heart has gone, there follows my hand,
   and not elsewhere.   50
For when the heart goes before, like a lamp, and il-
   lumines the pathway,
Many things are made clear, that else lie hidden in
   darkness."
Thereupon the priest, her friend and father-confessor,
Said, with a smile, " O daughter! thy God thus speak-
   eth within thee!
Talk not of wasted affection, affection never was
   wasted;   55
If it enrich not the heart of another, its waters, returning
Back to their springs, like the rain, shall fill them full
   of refreshment;
That which the fountain sends forth returns again to
   the fountain.
Patience; accomplish thy labor; accomplish thy work
   of affection!
Sorrow and silence are strong, and patient endurance
   is godlike.   60

Therefore accomplish ' thy labor of love, till the heart
    is made godlike,
Purified, strengthened, perfected, and rendered more
    worthy of heaven ! "
Cheered by the good man's words, Evangeline labored
    and waited.
Still in her heart she heard the funeral dirge of the
    ocean,
But with its sound there was mingled a voice that
    whispered, "Despair not ! "   65
Thus did that poor soul wander in want and cheerless
    discomfort,
Bleeding, barefooted, over the shards and thorns of
    existence.
Let me essay, O Muse ! to follow the wanderer's foot-
    steps ; —
Not through each devious path, each changeful year of
    existence,
But as a traveller follows a streamlet's course through
    the valley :   70
Far from its margin at times, and seeing the gleam
    of its water
Here and there, in some open space, and at intervals only;
Then drawing nearer its banks, through sylvan glooms
    that conceal it,
Though he behold it not, he can hear its continuous
    murmur ;
Happy, at length, if he find the spot where it reaches
    an outlet.   75

II

IT was the month of May. Far down the Beautiful
River,
Past the Ohio shore and past the mouth of the Wabash,
Into the golden stream of the broad and swift Mis-
sissippi,
Floated a cumbrous boat, that was rowed by Acadian
boatmen.
It was a band of exiles : a raft, as it were, from the
shipwrecked   80
Nation, scattered along the coast, now floating together,
Bound by the bonds of a common belief and a common
misfortune ;
Men and women and children, who, guided by hope or
by hearsay,
Sought for their kith and their kin among the few-
acred farmers
On the Acadian coast, and the prairies of fair Ope-
lousas.   85
With them Evangeline went, and her guide, the Father
Felician.
Onward o'er sunken sands, through a wilderness sombre
with forests,
Day after day they glided adown the turbulent river;
Night after night, by their blazing fires, encamped on
its borders.
Now through rushing chutes, among green islands,
where plumelike   90

Cotton-trees nodded their shadowy crests, they swept
  with the current,
Then emerged into broad lagoons, where silvery sand-
  bars
Lay in the stream, and along the wimpling waves of
  their margin,
Shining with snow-white plumes, large flocks of pelicans waded.
Level the landscape grew, and along the shores of
  the river,   95
Shaded by china-trees, in the midst of luxuriant gar-
  dens,
Stood the houses of planters, with negro-cabins and
  dove-cots.
They were approaching the region where reigns perpetual summer,
Where through the Golden Coast, and groves of orange
  and citron,
Sweeps with majestic curve the river away to the
  eastward.   100
They, too, swerved from their course; and entering
  the Bayou of Plaquemine,
Soon were lost in a maze of sluggish and devious
  waters,
Which, like a network of steel, extended in every
  direction.
Over their heads the towering and tenebrous boughs
  of the cypress
Met in a dusky arch, and trailing mosses in mid-air

Waved like banners that hang on the walls of ancient
    cathedrals.   106
Deathlike the silence seemed, and unbroken, save by
    the herons
Home to their nests in the cedar-trees returning at
    sunset,
Or by the owl, as he greeted the moon with demoniac
    laughter.
Lovely the moonlight was as it glanced and gleamed
    on the water,   110
Gleamed on the columns of cypress and cedar sus-
    taining the arches,
Down through whose broken vaults it fell as through
    chinks in a ruin.
Dreamlike, and indistinct, and strange were all things
    around them;
And o'er their spirits there came a feeling of won-
    der and sadness, —
Strange forebodings of ill, unseen and that cannot be
    compassed.   115
As, at the tramp of a horse's hoof on the turf of
    the prairies,
Far in advance are closed the leaves of the shrinking
    mimosa,
So, at the hoof-beats of fate, with sad forebodings of evil,
Shrinks and closes the heart, ere the stroke of doom
    has attained it.
But Evangeline's heart was sustained by a vision,
    that faintly   ·   120

Floated before her eyes, and beckoned her on through
the moonlight.
It was the thought of her brain that assumed the
shape of a phantom.
Through those shadowy aisles had Gabriel wandered
before her,
And every stroke of the oar now brought him nearer
and nearer.

Then in his place, at the prow of the boat, rose one
of the oarsmen,   125
And, as a signal sound, if others like them peradventure
Sailed on those gloomy and midnight streams, blew a
blast on his bugle.
Wild through the dark colonnades and corridors leafy
the blast rang,
Breaking the seal of silence, and giving tongues to
the forest.
Soundless above them the banners of moss just stirred
to the music.   130
Multitudinous echoes awoke and died in the distance,
Over the watery floor, and beneath the reverberant
branches ;
But not a voice replied ; no answer came from the
darkness ;
And, when the echoes had ceased, like a sense of
pain was the silence.
Then Evangeline slept ; but the boatmen rowed
through the midnight,   135

Silent at times, then singing familiar Canadian boat-
songs,
Such as they sang of old ̈on their own Acadian rivers,
While through the night were heard the mysterious
sounds of the desert,
Far off, — indistinct, — as of wave or wind in the
forest,
Mixed with the whoop of the crane and the roar of
the grim alligator.   140

Thus ere another noon they emerged from the
shades; and before them
Lay in the golden sun, the lakes of the Atchafalaya.
Water-lilies in myriads rocked on the slight undula-
tions
Made by the passing oars, and, resplendent in beauty,
the lotus
Lifted her golden crown above the heads of the boatmen.   145
Faint was the air with the odorous breath of magnolia
blossoms,
And with the heat of noon; and numberless sylvan
islands,
Fragrant and thickly embowered with blossoming hedges
of roses,
Near to whose shores they glided along, invited to
slumber.
Soon by the fairest of these their weary oars were
suspended.   150

Under the boughs of Wachita willows, that grew by
the margin,
Safely their boat was moored; and scattered about
on the greensward,
Tired with their midnight toil, the weary travellers
slumbered.
Over them vast and high extended the cope of a cedar.
Swinging from its great arms, the trumpet-flower and
the grapevine   155
Hung their ladder of ropes aloft like the ladder of
Jacob,
On whose pendulous stairs the angels ascending, de-
scending,
Were the swift humming-birds, that flitted from blos-
som to blossom.
Such was the vision Evangeline saw as she slumbered
beneath it.
Filled was her heart with love, and the dawn of an
opening heaven   160
Lighted her soul in sleep with the glory of regions
celestial.

Nearer, and ever nearer, among the numberless
islands,
Darted a light, swift boat, that sped away o'er the water,
Urged on its course by the sinewy arms of hunters
and trappers.
Northward its prow was turned, to the land of the
bison and beaver.   165

At the helm sat a youth, with countenance thoughtful
and careworn.
Dark and neglected locks overshadowed his brow, and
a sadness
Somewhat beyond his years on his face was legibly
written.
Gabriel was it, who, weary with waiting, unhappy and
restless,
Sought in the Western wilds oblivion of self and of
sorrow.   170
Swiftly they glided along, close under the lee of the island,
But by the opposite bank, and behind a screen of
palmettos,
So that they saw not the boat, where it lay concealed
in the willows;
All undisturbed by the dash of their oars, and unseen,
were the sleepers.
Angel of God was there none to awaken the slumber-
ing maiden.   175
Swiftly they glided away, like the shade of a cloud
on the prairie.
After the sound of their oars on the tholes had died
in the distance,
As from a magic trance the sleepers awoke, and the
maiden
Said with a sigh to the friendly priest, "O Father
Felician !
Something says in my heart that near me Gabriel
wanders.   180

Is it a foolish dream, an idle and vague superstition ?
Or has an angel passed, and revealed the truth to my
  spirit ? "
Then, with a blush, she added, " Alas for my credulous
  fancy !
Unto ears like thine such words as these have no
  meaning."
But made answer the reverend man, and he smiled
  as he answered, —   185
" Daughter, thy words are not idle ; nor are they to
  me without meaning.
Feeling is deep and still ; and the word that floats on
  the surface
Is as the tossing buoy, that betrays where the anchor
  is hidden.
Therefore trust to thy heart, and to what the world
  calls illusions.
Gabriel truly is near thee ; for not far away to the
  southward,   190
On the banks of the Têche, are the towns of St. Maur
  and St. Martin.
There the long-wandering bride shall be given again
  to her bridegroom,
There the long-absent pastor regain his flock and his
  sheepfold.
Beautiful is the land, with its prairies and forests of
  fruit-trees ;
Under the feet a garden of flowers, and the bluest
  of heavens   195

Bending above, and resting its dome on the walls
    of the forest.
They who dwell there have named it the Eden of
    Louisiana."

With these words of cheer they arose and continued
    their journey.
Softly the evening came. The sun from the western
    horizon
Like a magician extended his golden wand o'er the
    landscape;   200
Twinkling vapors arose; and sky and water and forest
Seemed all on fire at the touch, and melted and
    mingled together.
Hanging between two skies, a cloud with edges of
    silver,
Floated the boat, with its dripping oars, on the mo-
    tionless water.
Filled was Evangeline's heart with inexpressible sweet-
   . ness.   205
Touched by the magic spell, the sacred fountains of
    feeling
Glowed with the light of love, as the skies and waters
    around her.
Then from a neighboring thicket the mocking bird,
    wildest of singers,
Swinging aloft on a willow spray that hung o'er the water,
Shook from his little throat such floods of delirious
    music,   210

That the whole air and the woods and the waves
    seemed silent to listen.   .

Plaintive at first were the tones and sad : then soar-
    ing to madness

Seemed they to follow or guide the revels of frenzied
    Bacchantes.

Single notes were then heard, in sorrowful, low lam-
    entation ;

Till, having gathered them all, he flung them abroad
    in derision,   215

As when, after a storm, a gust of wind through the
    tree-tops

Shakes down the rattling rain in a crystal shower
    on the branches.

With such a prelude as this, and hearts that throbbed
    with emotion,

Slowly they entered the Têche, where it flows through
    the green Opelousas,

And, through the amber air, above the crest of the
    woodland,   220

Saw the column of smoke that arose from a neigh-
    boring dwelling ; —

Sounds of a horn they heard, and the distant lowing
    of cattle.

III.

NEAR to the bank of the river, o'ershadowed by oaks,
    from whose branches

Garlands of Spanish moss and of mystic mistletoe
    flaunted,

Such as the Druids cut down with golden hatchets
   at Yule-tide,   225
Stood, secluded and still, the house of the herdsman.
   A garden
Girded it round about with a belt of luxuriant blos-
   soms,
Filling the air with fragrance. The house itself was
   of timbers
Hewn from the cypress-tree, and carefully fitted
   together.
. Large and low was the roof; and on slender columns
   supported,   230
Rose-wreathed, vine-encircled, a broad and spacious
   veranda,
Haunt of the humming-bird and the bee, extended
   around it.
At each end of the house, amid the flowers of the
   garden,
Stationed the dove-cots were, as love's perpetual
   symbol,
Scenes of endless wooing, and endless contentions of
   rivals.   .   235
Silence reigned o'er the place. The line of shadow
   and sunshine
Ran near the tops of the trees; but the house itself
   was in shadow,
And from its chimney-top, ascending and slowly ex-
   panding
Into the evening air, a thin blue column of smoke rose.

In the rear of the house, from the garden gate, ran
    a pathway   240
Through the great groves of oak to the skirts of the
    limitless prairie,
Into whose sea of flowers the sun was slowly de-
    scending.
Full in his track of light, like ships with shadowy
    canvas
Hanging loose from their spars in a motionless calm
    in the tropics,
Stood a cluster of trees, with tangled cordage of
    grape-vines.   245

    Just where the woodlands met the flowery surf of
    the prairie,
Mounted upon his horse, with Spanish saddle and
    stirrups,
Sat a herdsman, arrayed in gaiters and doublet of
    deerskin.
Broad and brown was the face that from under the
    Spanish sombrero
Gazed on the peaceful scene, with the lordly look of
    its master.   250
Round about him were numberless herds of kine, that
    were grazing
Quietly in the meadows, and breathing the vapory
    freshness
That uprose from the river, and spread itself over
    the landscape.

Slowly lifting the horn that hung at his side, and
    expanding
Fully his broad, deep chest, he blew a blast, that
    resounded   255
Wildly and sweet and far, through the still damp
    air of the evening.
Suddenly out of the grass the long white horns of
    the cattle
Rose like flakes of foam on the adverse currents of ocean.
Silent a moment they gazed, then bellowing rushed
    o'er the prairie,
And the whole mass became a cloud, a shade in the
    distance.   260
Then, as the herdsman turned to the house, through
    the gate of the garden
Saw he the forms of the priest and the maiden ad-
    vancing to meet him.
Suddenly down from his horse he sprang in amaze-
    ment, and forward
Rushed with extended arms and exclamations of
    wonder ;
When they beheld his face, they recognized Basil the
    blacksmith.   265
Hearty his welcome was, as he led his guests to the
    garden.
There in an arbor of roses with endless question and
    answer
Gave they vent to their hearts, and renewed their
    friendly embraces,

Laughing and weeping by turns, or sitting silent and
    thoughtful.
Thoughtful, for Gabriel came not; and now dark
    doubts and misgivings   270
Stole o'er the maiden's heart; and Basil, somewhat
    embarrassed,
Broke the silence and said, " If you came by the
    Atchafalaya,
How have you nowhere encountered my Gabriel's
    boat on the bayous ? "
Over Evangeline's face at the words of Basil a shade
    passed.
Tears came into her eyes, and she said, with a tremu-
    lous accent,   275
  " Gone ? is Gabriel gone? " and, concealing her face
    on his shoulder,
All her o'erburdened heart gave way, and she wept
    and lamented.
Then the good Basil said, — and his voice grew blithe
    as he said it, —
  " Be of good cheer, my child; it is only to-day he
    departed.
Foolish boy! he has left me alone with my herds
    and my horses.   280
Moody and restless grown, and tired and troubled,
    his spirit `
Could no longer endure the calm of this quiet ex-
    istence,
Thinking ever of thee, uncertain and sorrowful ever,

Ever silent, or speaking only of thee and his troubles,
He at length had become so tedious to men and to
   maidens,   285
Tedious even to me, that at length I bethought me,
   and sent him
Unto the town of Adayes to trade for mules with
   the Spaniards.
Thence he will follow the Indian trails to the Ozark
   Mountains,
Hunting for furs in the forests, on rivers trapping
   the beaver.
Therefore be of good cheer; we will follow the fugi-
   tive lover;   290
He is not far on his way, and the Fates and the
   streams are against him.
Up and away to-morrow, and through the red dew
   of the morning
We will follow him fast, and bring him back to his
   prison."

Then glad voices were heard, and up from the
   banks of the river,
Borne aloft on his comrades' arms, came Michael the
   fiddler.   295
Long under Basil's roof had he lived like a god on
   Olympus,
Having no other care than dispensing music to mortals.
Far renowned was he for his silver locks and his fiddle.
  "Long live Michael," they cried, "our brave Aca-
   dian minstrel!"

As they bore him aloft in triumphal procession; and
    straightway   300
Father Felician advanced with Evangeline, greeting
    the old man
Kindly and oft, and recalling the past, while Basil,
    enraptured,
Hailed with hilarious joy his old companions and
    gossips,
Laughing loud and long, and embracing mothers and
    daughters.
Much they marvelled to see the wealth of the ci-
    devant blacksmith,   305
All his domains and his herds, and his patriarchal
    demeanor;
Much they marvelled to hear his tales of the soil
    and the climate,
And of the prairies, whose numberless herds were
    his who would take them;
Each one thought in his heart, that he, too, would
    go and do likewise.
Thus they ascended the steps, and crossing the breezy
    veranda,   310
Entered the hall of the house, where already the
    supper of Basil
Waited his late return; and they rested and feasted
    together.

    Over the joyous feast the sudden darkness de-
    scended.

All was silent without, and, illuming the landscape
with silver,
Fair rose the dewy moon and the myriad stars ; but
within doors, 315
Brighter than these, shone the faces of friends in
the glimmering lamplight.
Then from his station aloft, at the head of the table,
the herdsman
Poured forth his heart and his wine together in endless profusion.
Lighting his pipe, that was filled with sweet Natchitoches tobacco,
Thus he spake to his guests, who listened, and smiled
as they listened : — 320
" Welcome once more, my friends, who long have
been friendless and homeless,
Welcome once more to a home, that is better per-
chance than the old one !
Here no hungry winter congeals our blood like the
rivers ;
Here no stony ground provokes the wrath of the
farmer.
Smoothly the ploughshare runs through the soil, as
a keel through the water. 325
All the year round the orange-groves are in blossom ;
and grass grows
More in a single night than a whole Canadian summer.
Here, too, numberless herds run wild and unclaimed
in the prairies ;

Here, too, lands may be had for the asking, and
    forests of timber
With a few blows of the axe are hewn and framed
    into houses.   330
After your houses are built, and your fields are yellow
    with harvests,
No King George of England shall drive you away
    from your homesteads,
Burning your dwellings and barns, and stealing your
    farms and your cattle."
Speaking these words, he blew a wrathful cloud from
    his nostrils,
While his huge, brown hand came thundering down
    on the table,   335
So that the guests all started; and Father Felician,
    astounded,
Suddenly paused, with a pinch of snuff half-way to
    his nostrils.
But the brave Basil resumed, and his words were
    milder and gayer : —
"Only beware of the fever, my friends, beware of
    the fever !
For it is not like that of our cold Acadian climate, 340
Cured by wearing a spider hung round one's neck
    in a nutshell ! "
Then there were voices heard at the door, and foot-
    steps approaching
Sounded upon the stairs and the floor of the breezy
    veranda.

It was the neighboring Creoles and small Acadian
  planters,
Who had been summoned all to the house of Basil
  the Herdsman.   345
Merry the meeting was of ancient comrades and
  neighbors :
Friend clasped friend in his arms ; and they who
  before were as strangers,
Meeting in exile, became straightway as friends to
  each other,
Drawn by the gentle bond of a common country
  together.
But in the neighboring hall a strain of music, pro-
  ceeding   350
From the accordant strings of Michael's melodious fiddle,
Broke up all further speech. Away, like children
  delighted,
All things forgotten beside, they gave themselves to
  the maddening
Whirl of the giddy dance, as it swept and swayed
  to the music,
Dreamlike, with beaming eyes and the rush of flut-
  tering garments.   355

Meanwhile, apart, at the head of the hall, the priest
  and the herdsman   ˴
Sat, conversing together of past and present and future ;
While Evangeline stood like one entranced, for within
  her

Olden memories rose, and loud in the midst of the music
Heard she the sound of the sea, and an irrepressible
    sadness   360
Came o'er her heart, and unseen she stole forth into
    the garden.
Beautiful was the night.   Behind the black wall of
    the forest,
Tipping its summit with silver, arose the moon.   On
    the river
Fell here and there through the branches a tremulous
    gleam of the moonlight,
Like the sweet thoughts of love on a darkened and
    devious spirit.   365
Nearer and round about her, the manifold flowers of
    the garden
Poured out their souls in odors, that were their prayers
    and confessions
Unto the night, as it went its way, like a silent
    Carthusian.
Fuller of fragrance than they, and as heavy with
    shadows and night-dews,
Hung the heart of the maiden.   The calm and the
    magical moonlight   370
Seemed to inundate her soul with indefinable longings,
As, through the garden-gate, and beneath the shade
    of the oak-trees,
Passed she along the path to the edge of the meas-
    ureless prairie.
Silent it lay, with a silvery haze upon it, and fire-flies

Gleamed and floated away in mingled and infinite
    numbers.   375
Over her head the stars, the thoughts of God in the
    heavens,
Shone on the eyes of man, who had ceased to marvel
    and worship,
Save when a blazing comet was seen on the walls of
    that temple,
As if a hand had appeared and written upon them,
    " Upharsin."
And the soul of the maiden, between the stars and
    the fire-flies,   380
Wandered alone, and she cried, "O Gabriel! O my
    beloved!
Art thou so near unto me, and yet I cannot behold
    thee ?
Art thou so near unto me, and yet thy voice does
    not reach me ?
Ah! how often thy feet have trod this path to the
    prairie !
Ah! how often thine eyes have looked on the wood-
    lands around me !   385
Ah! how often beneath this oak, returning from labor,
Thou hast lain down to rest, and to dream of me
    in thy slumbers !
When shall these eyes behold, these arms be folded
    about thee ? "
Loud and sudden and near the notes of a whippoor-
    will sounded

Like a flute in the woods; and anon, through the
    neighboring thickets,   390
Farther and farther away it floated and dropped into
    silence.
    " Patience!" whispered the oaks from oracular cav-
    erns of darkness :
And, from the moonlit meadow, a sigh responded,
    "To-morrow!"

    Bright rose the sun next day; and all the flowers
    of the garden
Bathed his shining feet with their tears, and anointed
    his tresses   395
With the delicious balm that they bore in their vases
    of crystal.
    " Farewell!" said the priest, as he stood at the
    shadowy threshold ;
    " See that you bring us the Prodigal Son from his
    fasting and famine,
And, too, the Foolish Virgin, who slept when the
    bridegroom was coming."
    " Farewell!" answered the maiden, and, smiling,
    with Basil descended   400
Down to the river's brink, where the boatmen already
    were waiting.
Thus beginning their journey with morning, and sun-
    shine, and gladness,
Swiftly they followed the flight of him who was speed-
    ing before them,

Blown by the blast of fate like a dead leaf over the
    desert.
Not that day, nor the next, nor yet the day that
    succeeded,   405
Found they the trace of his course, in lake or forest
    or river,
Nor, after many days, had they found him ; but vague
    and uncertain
Rumors alone were their guides through a wild and
    desolate country ;
Till, at the little inn of the Spanish town of Adayes,
Weary and worn, they alighted, and learned from the
    garrulous landlord,   410
That on the day before, with horses and guides and
    companions,
Gabriel left the village, and took the road of the
    prairies.

IV.

Far in the West there lies a desert land, where the
    mountains
Lift, through perpetual snows, their lofty and lumi-
    nous summits.
Down from their jagged, deep ravines, where the gorge,
    like a gateway,   415
Opens a passage rude to the wheels of the emigrant's
    wagon,
Westward the Oregon flows and the Walleway and
    Owyhee.

Eastward, with devious course, among the Wind-river
  Mountains,
Through the Sweet-water Valley precipitate leaps the
  Nebraska ;
And to the south, from Fontaine-qui-bout and the
  Spanish sierras,   420
Fretted with sands and rocks, and swept by the wind
  of the desert,
Numberless torrents, with ceaseless sound, descend to
  the ocean,
Like the great chords of a harp, in loud and solemn
  vibrations.
Spreading between these streams are the wondrous,
  beautiful prairies ;
Billowy bays of grass ever rolling in shadow and sun-
  shine,   425
Bright with luxuriant clusters of roses and purple
  amorphas.
Over them wandered the buffalo herds, and the elk
  and the roebuck ;
Over them wandered the wolves, and herds of rider-
  less horses ;
Fires that blast and blight, and winds that are weary
  with travel ;
Over them wander the scattered tribes of Ishmael's
  children,   430
Staining the desert with blood ; and above their terrible
  war-trails
Circles and sails aloft, on pinions majestic, the vulture,

Like the implacable soul of a chieftain slaughtered
   in battle,
By invisible stairs ascending and scaling the heavens.
Here and there rise smokes from the camps of these
   savage marauders ;   435
Here and there rise groves from the margins of swift-
   running rivers ;
And the grim, taciturn bear, the anchorite monk of
   the desert,
Climbs down their dark ravines to dig for roots by
   the brook-side,
And over all is the sky, the clear and crystalline
   heaven,
Like the protecting hand of God inverted above them.

Into this wonderful land, at the base of the Ozark
   Mountains,
Gabriel ·far had entered, with hunters and trappers
   behind him.
Day after day, with their Indian guides, the maiden
   and Basil
Followed his flying steps, and thought each day to·
   o'ertake him.
Sometimes they saw, or thought they saw, the smoke
   of his camp-fire   445
Rise in the morning air from the distant plain ; but
   at nightfall,
When they had reached the place they found only
   embers and ashes.

And, though their hearts were sad at times and their
    bodies were weary,
Hope still guided them on, as the magic Fata Morgana
Showed them her lakes of light, that retreated and
    vanished before them.   450

   Once, as they sat by their evening fire, there silently
    entered
Into their little camp an Indian woman, whose features,
Wore deep traces of sorrow, and patience as great as
    her sorrow.
She was a Shawnee woman returning home to her
    people,
From the far-off hunting-grounds of the cruel Ca-
    manches,   455
Where her Canadian husband, a Coureur-des-Bois, had
    been murdered.
Touched were their hearts at her story, and warmest
    and friendliest welcome
Gave they, with words of cheer, and she sat and
    feasted among them
On the buffalo-meat and the venison cooked on the
    embers.
But when their meal was done, and Basil and all
    his companions,   460
Worn with the long day's march and the chase of
    the deer and the bison,
Stretched themselves on the ground, and slept where
    the quivering fire-light

Flashed on their swarthy cheeks, and their forms
  wrapped up in their blankets,
Then at the door of Evangeline's tent she sat and
  repeated.
Slowly, with soft, low voice, and the charm of her
  Indian accent, 465
All the tale of her love, with its pleasures, and pains,
  and reverses.
Much Evangeline wept at the tale, and to know that
  another
Hapless heart like her own had loved and had been
  disappointed.
Moved to the depths of her soul by pity and woman's
  compassion,
Yet in her sorrow pleased that one who had suffered
  was near her, 470
She in turn related her love and all its disasters.
Mute with wonder the Shawnee sat, and when she
  had ended
Still was mute; but at length, as if a mysterious
  horror
Passed through her brain, she spake, and repeated
  the tale of the Mowis;
Mowis, the bridegroom of snow, who won and wedded
  a maiden, 475
But, when the morning came, arose and passed from
  the wigwam,
Fading and melting away and dissolving into the sun-
  shine,

Till she beheld him no more, though she followed
    far into the forest.

Then, in those sweet, low tones, that seemed like a
    weird incantation,

Told she the tale of the fair Lilinau, who was wooed
    by a phantom,   480

That through the pines o'er her father's lodge, in the
    hush of the twilight,

Breathed like the evening wind, and whispered love
    to the maiden,

Till she followed his green and waving plume through
    the forest,

And nevermore returned, nor was seen again by her
    people.

Silent with wonder and strange surprise, Evangeline
    listened   485

To the soft flow of her magical words, till the region
    around her

Seemed like enchanted ground, and her swarthy guest
    the enchantress.

Slowly over the tops of the Ozark Mountains the moon
    rose,

Lighting the little tent, and with a mysterious splendor

Touching the sombre leaves, and embracing and filling
    the woodland.   490

With a delicious sound the brook rushed by, and the
    branches

Swayed and sighed overhead in scarcely audible whis-
    pers.

Filled with the thoughts of love was Evangeline's
heart, but a secret,
Subtle sense crept in of pain and indefinite terror,
As the cold, poisonous snake creeps into the nest of
the swallow.   495
It was no earthly fear. A breath from the region
of spirits
Seemed to float in the air of night; and she felt
for a moment
That, like the Indian maid, she, too, was pursuing
a phantom.
With this thought she slept, and the fear and the
phantom had vanished.

Early upon the morrow the march was resumed;
and the Shawnee   500
Said, as they journeyed along, " On the western slope
of these mountains
Dwells in his little village the Black Robe chief of
the Mission.
Much he teaches the people, and tells them of Mary
and Jesus.
Loud laugh their hearts with joy, and weep with
pain, as they hear him."
Then, with a sudden and secret emotion, Evangeline
answered,   505
" Let us go to the Mission, for there good tidings
await us ! "
Thither they turned their steeds ; and behind a spur
of the mountains.

Just as the sun went down, they heard a murmur
 of voices,
And in a meadow green and broad, by the bank of
 a river,
Saw the tents of the Christians, the tents of the Jesuit
 Mission.   510
Under a towering oak, that stood in the midst of the
 village,
Knelt the Black Robe chief with his children. A
 crucifix fastened
High on the trunk of the tree, and overshadowed
 by grapevines,
Looked with its agonized face on the multitude kneel-
 ing beneath it.
This was their rural chapel. Aloft, through the in-
 tricate arches   515
Of its aerial roof, arose the chant of their vespers,
Mingling its notes with the soft susurrus and sighs
 of the branches.
Silent, with heads uncovered, the travellers, nearer
 approaching,
Knelt on the swarded floor, and joined in the evening devotions.
But when the service was done, and the benediction
 had fallen   520
Forth from the hands of the priest, like seed from
 the hands of the sower,
Slowly the reverend man advanced to the strangers,
 and bade them

Welcome; and when they replied, he smiled with
    benignant expression,
Hearing the homelike sounds of his mother-tongue in
    the forest,
And, with words of kindness, conducted them into
    his wigwam.   525
There upon mats and skins they reposed, and on cakes
    of the maize-ear
Feasted, and slaked their thirst from the water-gourd
    of the teacher.
Soon was their story told; and the priest with solem-
    nity answered : —
"Not six suns have risen and set since Gabriel,
    seated
On this mat by my side, where now the maiden reposes,
Told me this same sad tale; then arose and continued
    his journey!"
Soft was the voice of the priest, and he spake with
    an accent of kindness;
But on Evangeline's heart fell his words as in winter
    the snow-flakes
Fall into some lone nest from which the birds have
    departed.
"Far to the north he has gone," continued the priest;
    but in autumn,   535
When the chase is done, will return again to the
    Mission."
Then Evangeline said, and her voice was meek and
    submissive,

" Let me remain with thee, for my soul is sad and
    afflicted."
So seemed it wise and well unto all; and betimes
    on the morrow,
Mounting his Mexican steed, with his Indian guides
    and companions,   540
Homeward Basil returned, and Evangeline stayed at
    the Mission.

Slowly, slowly, slowly the days succeeded each
    other, —
Days and weeks and months; and the fields of maize
    that were springing
Green from the ground when a stranger she came,
    now waving above her,
Lifted their slender shafts, with leaves interlacing, and
    forming   545
Cloisters for mendicant crows and granaries pillaged
    by squirrels.
Then in the golden weather the maize was husked,
    and the maidens
Blushed at each blood-red ear, for that betokened a lover,
But at the crooked laughed, and called it a thief in
    the corn-field.
Even the blood-red ear to Evangeline brought not her
    lover.   550
" Patience ! " the priest would say; " have faith, and
    thy prayer will be answered !
Look at this vigorous plant that lifts its head from
    the meadow,

See how its leaves are turned to the north, as true
    as the magnet;
This is the compass-flower, that the finger of God
    has planted
Here in the houseless wild, to direct the traveller's
    journey   ·   555
Over the sea-like, pathless, limitless waste of the
    desert.
Such in the soul of man is faith. The blossoms of
    passion,
Gay and luxuriant flowers, are brighter and fuller
    of fragrance,
But they beguile us, and lead us astray, and their
    odor is deadly.
Only this humble plant can guide us here, and here-
    after   560
Crown us with asphodel flowers, that are wet with
    the dews of nepenthe."

So came the autumn, and passed, and the winter,
    — yet Gabriel came not;
Blossomed the opening spring, and the notes of the
    robbin and bluebird
Sounded sweet upon wold and in wood, yet Gabriel
    came not.
But on the breath of the summer winds a rumor was
    wafted   565
Sweeter than song of bird, or hue or odor of blossom.
Far to the north and east, it said, in the Michigan forests,

Gabriel had his lodge by the banks of the Saginaw
    River.

And, with returning guides, that sought the lakes of
    St. Lawrence,

Saying a sad farewell, Evangeline went from the
    Mission.   570

When over weary ways, by long and perilous marches,

She had attained at length the depths of the Michigan
    forests,

Found she the hunter's lodge deserted and fallen to
    ruin !

    Thus did the long sad years glide on, and in sea-
    sons and places

Divers and distant far was seen the wandering
    maiden ; —   575

Now in the Tents of Grace of the meek Moravian
    Missions,

Now in the noisy camps and the battle-fields of the
    army,

Now in secluded hamlets, in towns and populous cities.

Like a phantom she came, and passed away unremem-
    bered.

Fair was she and young, when in hope began the
    long journey;   580

Faded was she and old, when in disappointment it
    ended.

Each succeeding year stole something away from her
    beauty,

Leaving behind it, broader and deeper, the gloom and
the shadow.
Then there appeared and spread faint streaks of gray
o'er her forehead,
Dawn of another life, that broke o'er her earthly
horizon,   585
As in the eastern sky the first faint streaks of the
morning.

V.

In that delightful land which is washed by the Dela-
ware waters,
Guarding in sylvan shades the name of Penn the
apostle,
Stands on the banks of its beautiful stream the city
he founded.
There all the air is balm, and the peach is the emblem
of beauty,   590
And the streets still reëcho the names of the trees
of the forest,
As if they fain would appease the Dryads whose haunts
they molested.
There from the troubled sea had Evangeline landed,
an exile,
Finding among the children of Penn a home and a
country.
There old René Leblanc had died; and when he
departed,   595

Saw at his side only one of all his hundred descend-
ants.

Something at least there was in the friendly streets
of the city,

Something that spake to her heart, and made her no
longer a stranger;

And her ear was pleased with the Thee and Thou
of the Quakers,

For it recalled the past, the old Acadian country, 600

Where all men were equal, and all were brothers and
sisters.

So, when the fruitless search, the disappointed endeavor,

Ended, to recommence no more upon earth, uncom-
plaining,

Thither, as leaves to the light, were turned her
thoughts and her footsteps.

As from the mountain's top the rainy mists of the
morning   605

Roll away, and afar we behold the landscape below
us,

Sun-illumined, with shining rivers and cities and
hamlets,

So fell the mists from her mind, and she saw the
world far below her,

Dark no longer, but all illumined with love; and the
pathway

Which she had climbed so far, lying smooth and fair
in the distance.   610

Gabriel was not forgotten. Within her heart was his
image,
Clothed in the beauty of love and youth, as last she
beheld him,
Only more beautiful made by his death-like silence
and absence.
Into her thoughts of him time entered not, for it
was not.
Over him years had no power; he was not changed,
but transfigured;   615
He had become in her heart as one who is dead,
and not absent;
Patience and abnegation of self, and devotion to others,
This was the lesson a life of trial and sorrow had
taught her.
So was her love diffused, but, like to some odorous
spices,
Suffered no waste nor loss, though filling the air with
aroma.   620
Other hope had she none, nor wish in life, but to
follow
Meekly, with reverent steps, the sacred feet of her
Saviour.
Thus many years she lived as a Sister of Mercy;
frequenting
Lonely and wretched roofs in the crowded lanes of
the city,
Where distress and want concealed themselves from
the sunlight,   625

Where disease and sorrow in garrets languished neglected.
Night after night, when the world was asleep, as the
watchman repeated
Loud, through the gusty streets, that all was well
in the city,
High at some lonely window he saw the light of her
taper.
Day after day, in the gray of the dawn, as slow
through the suburbs   630
Plodded the German farmer, with flowers and fruits
for the market,
Met he that meek, pale face, returning home from
its watchings.

Then it came to pass that a pestilence fell on the
city,
Presaged by wondrous signs, and mostly by flocks of
wild pigeons,
Darkening the sun in their flight, with naught in
their claws but an acorn.   635
And, as the tides of the sea arise in the month of
September,
Flooding some silver stream, till it spreads to a lake
in the meadow,
So death flooded life, and, o'erflowing its natural
margin,
Spread to a brackish lake, the silver stream of ex-
istence.

Wealth had no power to bribe, nor beauty to charm,
the oppressor ;   640
But all perished alike beneath the scourge of his
anger ; —
Only, alas ! the poor, who had neither friends nor
attendants,
Crept away to die in the almshouse, home of the
homeless.
Then in the suburbs it stood, in the midst of mead-
ows and woodlands ; —
Now the city surrounds it ; but still, with its gateway
and wicket .   645
Meek, in the midst of splendor, its humble walls
seemed to echo
Softly the words of the Lord : " The poor ye always
have with you."
Thither, by night and by day, came the Sister of
Mercy. The dying
Looked up into her face, and thought, indeed, to behold
there
Gleams of celestial light encircle her forehead with
splendor,   650
Such as the artist paints o'er the brows of saints
and apostles,
Or such as hangs by night o'er a city seen at a dis-
tance.
Unto their eyes it seemed the lamps of the city celestial,
Into whose shining gates erelong their spirits would
enter.

Thus, on a Sabbath morn, through the streets, de-
    serted and silent,   655
Wending her quiet way, she entered the door of the
    almshouse.
Sweet on the summer air was the odor of flowers
    in the garden;
And she paused on her way to gather the fairest
    among them,
That the dying once more might rejoice in their fra-
    grance and beauty.
Then, as she mounted the stairs to the corridors, cooled
    by the east-wind,   660
Distant and soft on her ear fell the chimes from the
    belfry of Christ Church,
While, intermingled with these, across the meadows
    were wafted
Sounds of psalms, that were sung by the Swedes in
    their church at Wicaco.
Soft as descending wings fell the calm of the hour
    on her spirit:
Something within her said, "At length thy trials are
    ended;"   665
And, with light in her looks, she entered the chambers
    of sickness.
Noiselessly moved about the assiduous, careful attend-
    ants,
Moistening the feverish lip, and the aching brow, and
    in silence

Closing the sightless eyes of the dead, and concealing
    their faces,
Where on their pallets they lay, like drifts of snow
    by the roadside. 670
Many a languid head, upraised as Evangeline entered,
Turned on its pillow of pain to gaze while she passed,
    for her presence
Fell on their hearts like a ray of the sun on the walls
    of a prison.
And, as she looked around, she saw how Death, the
    consoler,
Laying his hand upon many a heart, had healed it
    forever. 675
Many familiar forms had disappeared in the night
    time ;
Vacant their places were, or filled already by strangers.

Suddenly, as if arrested by fear or a feeling of
    wonder,
Still she stood, with her colorless lips apart, while
    a shudder
Ran through her frame, and, forgotten, the flowerets
    dropped from her fingers, 680
And from her eyes and cheeks the light and bloom
    of the morning.
Then there escaped from her lips a cry of such terri-
    ble anguish,
That the dying heard it, and started up from their
    pillows.

On the pallet before her was stretched the form of
an old man.

Long, and thin, and gray were the locks that shaded
his temples;   685

But, as he lay in the morning light, his face for a
moment

Seemed to assume once more the forms of its earlier
manhood;

So are wont to be changed the faces of those who
are dying.

Hot and red on his lips still burned the flush of the fever,

As if life, like the Hebrew, with blood had besprinkled
its portals,   690

That the Angel of Death might see the sign, and
pass over.

Motionless, senseless, dying, he lay, and his spirit
exhausted

Seemed to be sinking down through infinite depths
in the darkness,

Darkness of slumber and death, forever sinking and
sinking.

Then through those realms of shade, in multiplied
reverberations,   695

Heard he that cry of pain, and through the hush
that succeeded

Whispered a gentle voice, in accents tender and saint-
like,

   "Gabriel! O my beloved!" and died away into
silence.

Then he beheld, in a dream, once more the home
  of his childhood ;
Green Acadian meadows, with sylvan rivers among
  them,
Village, and mountain, and woodlands ; and, walking
  under their shadow, 700
As in the days of her youth, Evangeline rose in his
  vision.
Tears came into his eyes ; and as slowly he lifted
  his eyelids,
Vanished the vision away, but Evangeline knelt by
  his bedside.
Vainly he strove to whisper her name, for the accents
  unuttered
Died on his lips, and their motion revealed what his
  tongue would have spoken. 705
Vainly he strove to rise ; and Evangeline, kneeling
  beside him,
Kissed his dying lips, and laid his head on her bosom.
Sweet was the light of his eyes ; but it suddenly sank
  into darkness,
As when a lamp is blown out by a gust of wind at
  a casement.

All was ended now, the hope, and the fear, and
  the sorrow, 710
All the aching of heart, the restless, unsatisfied longing,
All the dull, deep pain, and constant anguish of
  patience !

And, as she pressed once more the lifeless head to
    her bosom,
Meekly she bowed her own, and murmured, "Father,
    I thank thee!"

STILL stands the forest primeval; but far away from
    its shadow,
Side by side, in their nameless graves, the lovers are
    sleeping.
Under the humble walls of the little Catholic church-
    yard,
In the heart of the city, they lie, unknown and un-
    noticed.
Daily the tides of life go ebbing and flowing beside
    them,   5
Thousands of throbbing hearts, where theirs are at
    rest and forever,
Thousands of aching brains, where theirs no longer
    are busy,
Thousands of toiling hands, where theirs have ceased
    from their labors,
Thousands of weary feet, where theirs have completed
    their journey!

    Still stands the forest primeval; but under the shade
        of its branches   10

Dwells another race, with other customs and language.
Only along the shore of the mournful and misty
  Atlantic
Linger a few Acadian peasants, whose fathers from
  exile
Wandered back to their native land to die in its bosom.
In the fisherman's cot the wheel and the loom are still
  busy;   15
Maidens still wear their Norman caps and their kirtles
  of homespun,
And by the evening fire repeat Evangeline's story,
While from its rocky caverns the deep-voiced, neighbor-
  ing ocean
Speaks, and in accents disconsolate answers the wail
  of the forest.

LITERARY ESTIMATES OF THE POET.

LONGFELLOW'S GOLDEN LEGEND.

Blackwood's Magazine, February, 1852.

"No man can read six pages of *The Golden Legend*, without being reminded of the *Faust*, and that so strongly that there is a perpetual challenge of comparison. So long as the popularity of the elder poem continues, the later one must suffer in consequence.

"Whether Mr. Longfellow could have avoided this, is quite another question. We confess that we entertain very great doubts as to that point. In respect of melody, feeling, pathos, and that exquisite simplicity of expression which is the criterion of a genuine poet, Mr. Longfellow need not shun comparison with any living writer. He is not only by nature a poet, but he has cultivated his poetical powers to the utmost. No man, we really believe, has bestowed more pains upon poetry than he has. He has studied rhythm most thoroughly; he has subjected the most beautiful strains of the masters of verbal melody, in many languages, to a minute and careful analysis; he has arrived at his poetical theories by dint of long and thoughtful investigation; and yet, exquisite as the product is which he has now given us, there is a large portion of it which we cannot style as truly original."

AMERICAN LITERATURE.

CHARLES F. RICHARDSON.

"The chief value of *Evangeline* as a metrical experiment was limited, but great: it proved that English hexameters were best fitted for idyllic, rather than Homeric, narrative."

"But Longfellow's best hexameters, in *Evangeline*, though representing neither the force nor the flexibility of the Greek measure of the same name, had a genuine musical beauty of their own."

ESSAYS AND REVIEWS.

EDWIN P. WHIPPLE.

"His [Longfellow's] sense of beauty, though uncommonly vivid, is not the highest of which the mind is capable. He has little conception of its mysterious spirit ; — of that Beauty, of which all physical loveliness is but the shadow, which awes and thrills the soul into which it enters, and lifts the imagination into regions 'to which the heaven of heavens is but a veil.' His mind never appears oppressed, nor his sight dimmed, by its exceeding glory. He feels, and loves, and creates, what is beautiful ; but he hymns no reverence, he pays no adoration, to the Spirit of Beauty. He would never exclaim with Shelley, 'O awful Loveliness ! ' "

"The sympathies which Longfellow addresses are fine and poetical, but not the most subtle of which the soul is capable. The kindly affections, the moral sentiments, the joys, sorrows, regrets, aspirations, loves, and wishes of the heart, he has consecrated by new ideal forms and ascriptions."

DEVELOPMENT OF ENGLISH LITERATURE AND LANGUAGE.

WELSH.

"In extent of popularity, the central figure in American poetry. In respect of airy grace, elegance, melody, pathos, naturalness, he stands unsurpassed, if not unequalled, among the poets of the age. In scholarship, in polite culture, he must be classed among the learned; yet he has not the strong pinion to dive into the abyss of thought, or soar into the empyrean of speculation. He does not approach the concentration and intensity of the grand masters, nor their dramatic movement and variety. He is not the bard of passion, as Byron; nor of ideality, as Shelley; nor of high contemplation, as Wordsworth; but of daily life, familiar experience, domestic affection."

"Like Hawthorne, but without his intense imagination, he had a genuine fondness for the mellow, the distant, the old. His poems indicate the region of his habitual thought, — the legendary of the Old World or the New. The man is more than his work."

NOTES.

PROLOGUE.

THERE is a fine, emotional quality in the prologue. It suggests the preludes of Sir Walter Scott to the cantos of *The Lay of the Last Minstrel*; it has not, however, the personal quality well suited, indeed, to introduce " customs and manners anciently prevailing on the Borders." The lay gives a bardic feudal picture to which its octo-syllabic measure is admirably adapted. The *Evangeline* prologue invests the primeval Acadian forest with a grand but idyllic dignity, while the stately hexameters in which the poem is written lend a kind of Homeric charm to the theme announced in the first two lines of the last of the three stanzas of uneven length : —

" Ye who believe in affection that hopes, and endures, and is patient,
 Ye who believe in the beauty and strength of woman's devotion."

Acadia. This term originally embraced all the land between the sites of Philadelphia and Montreal; afterwards it was limited to New Brunswick and the adjacent islands; now it is a synonym for Nova Scotia.

Druids. Priests of Ancient Gaul and Britain.

Eld. An archaic term used in poetry. Druids of eld = Druids of old.

Hexameter verse consists of six feet which may be either dactyls or spondees. The dactyl consists of one accented and two unaccented syllables. The spondee has two accented syllables. A trochee may take the place of a spondee. A trochee consists of an accented and an unaccented syllable, as cúrfew. Accented and unaccented syllables in English are the corresponding terms for long and short syllables in Greek and Latin. Hexameter, whether classical or English, employs the dactyl as the unit of rhythm; in this verse, the fifth foot is usually a dactyl, the sixth, a spondee or trochee.

English hexameter is easy to write poorly, and difficult to write with the sonorous, measured rhythm of the classical hexameter. This is because the English language has few syllables of even quantity which can be used contiguously. It is, therefore, in the use of the spondee, that English hexameter is conspicuously weak. As an example of a spondaic line which is particularly fine, notice the fourth verse of the first stanza of the prelude : —

Stand like | harpers | hoar, with | beards that | rest on their | bosoms.

Let the student, as an exercise, notice how often, in a single canto, the dactyl falls in the fifth foot. A canto of a poem is like a chapter in prose. A canto is a group of stanzas; a chapter is a group of paragraphs. Each serves to develop one scene or a series of allied thoughts and situations. The cantos in *Evangeline* are indicated by Roman numerals.

Longfellow was much criticised for writing *Evangeline* in hexameters. Oliver Wendell Holmes approved of the metre. The poem was published on Oct. 30, 1847.

Judging from the prologue, what was the poet's favorite rhetorical figure? Mention a Roman and an Elizabethan poet who freely employed the same figure.

PART THE FIRST.

I.

THE first stanza of *Part the First* is devoted to a description of Grand-Pré, its environment and its inhabitants. The theme, *Evangeline*, is introduced in the second stanza.

Grand-Pré = great meadow.

Basin of Minas. " A remarkable body of water in Nova Scotia, the east arm of the Bay of Fundy, penetrating sixty miles inland." " The tides here rush in with great impetuosity and form what is called the *bore*. At the equinoxes they have been known to rise from sixty to seventy feet." The editor found it deeply interesting to watch steamboats unload at the little towns on the Basin of Minas. Although many hands made light work, and freight was landed with great dexterity and quickness, the tide rose so rapidly that the sloping stationary bridges built to accommodate the water at all heights were buried many feet in the few minutes spent at each stopping-place. For an interesting episode descriptive of the tide on the Basin, read I. Zangwill's *The Master*.

10. Blomidon. One of the Cobequid range which runs through the interior of Nova Scotia.

15. Reign of the Henries ; i.e., in the Sixteenth Century.

20. Kirtles. A garment, whether short or long, with a skirt. — *Standard Dictionary*.

21. Distaffs. See *Europe in the Nineteenth Century*, Chap. xxviii., "Progress of the World" (JUDSON).

23. Whir of the wheels. For a clear and concise account of alliteration, both as rhyme and as regards its history, read *English Versification*, Chap. vii. (PARSONS).

30. Angelus. A devotion commemorating the Annunciation. A bell rung as in Roman Catholic custom, at morning, noon, and night, as a call to recite the *angelus*, or to give notice of the hour when it is recited. — *Standard Dictionary*.

34. Let class begin with verse 34 and read aloud to end of stanza. Notice cæsural pause of verse 34. Notice how accent is thrust on *locks* in line 36. *But their dwellings*, etc., is an example of how easily hexameter may degenerate into prose. For explanation of cæsural pause, see *English Versification*, page 71.

43. Stalworth. [Archaic.] Stalwart.

What beautiful metaphor in second stanza describes Benedict Bellefontaine?

53. Hyssop. 1. A bushy herb of the mint family. 2. An unidentified plant furnishing the twigs used in the Mosaic purificatory and sacrificial rites, etc.; thought by some to have been a species of marjoram. — *Standard Dictionary*.

Is hyssop in the text employed literally or figuratively?

55. Chaplet. The third part of a rosary; i.e., fifty-five beads.

55. Missal. A mass-book.

56. Norman cap. In color, white; in shape, with a high point above the face.

What verse, beautiful in sound and sense, in stanza second, suggests harmony between Evangeline's character and appearance?

64. Did the hill command the open sea ?

65. **Sycamore.** The buttonwood.

68. **Penthouse.** Shield projecting above a window or door to protect from the weather.

74. **Wains.** [Archaic.] Wagons.

74. **Antique ploughs.** The plough is of great antiquity. It is mentioned in Hesiod's *Works and Days.*

What verse in the third stanza is prophetic of coming disaster ?

In stanza fourth Basil the blacksmith is drawn with the same tenderness with which the poet portrays " The Village Blacksmith " in the poem bearing that title.

Has the blacksmith classic celebrity ?

103. **Plain-song.** "A name given to the ecclesiastical chant by the Church of Rome. It is an extremely simple melody, admitting only notes of equal value, rarely extending beyond the compass of an octave, and never exceeding nine notes, the staff on which the notes are placed consisting of only four lines. . . . St. Ambrose is considered to have been the inventor or systematiser of plainsong." — *Chambers's Encyclopædia.*

114. Who were " **nuns** "? — the children or the sparks ?

120. **Stone in the nest of the swallow.** A pebble anciently supposed to be brought from the seashore by swallows, and fed to their young to make them see. — *Standard Dictionary.*

122. What god in Greek mythology is suggested by this line ?

125. **Saint Eulalie.** A saint of the Roman Church, born in Spain in 290. Both Merida and Barcelona claim her relics. History would indicate that she was pugnacious. Of pugnacity, Longfellow probably did not think. His poetic ear was doubtless set to vibrating with the music of the saint's name.

128. How many spondees are there in this line ?

Notice the poetic beauty of the names thus far introduced. Pupils should pronounce in succession, Benedict Bellefontaine, Gabriel Lajeunesse, Father Felician, Evangeline, Saint Eulalie; they should count the vowels and liquids in each of these names.

What great modern French writer made sound as indicative of sense a life-long study ? Mention his two greatest novels ? Which of these was represented by a celebrated painting in the French department at the World's Fair ?

What is the name of a modern school of French writers who pay great attention to the sound of words as indicative of meaning ?

II.

130. **And the retreating sun the sign of the Scorpion enters.** See *Chambers's Encyclopædia* on *Zodiac.* See also *Encyclopædia Britannica.* The Zodiac is "an imaginary zone of the heavens, within which lie the paths of the sun, moon, and principal planets." "It is divided into twelve signs, and marked by twelve constellations." These signs are Aries, Taurus, Gemini, Cancer, Leo, Virgo, Libra, Scorpio, Sagittarius, Capricornus, Aquarius, and Pisces. "The definitive decline of the sun's power after the autumnal equinox was typified by placing a scorpion as the symbol of darkness in the eighth sign."

134. Notice the beauty of the simile.

140. **Summer of All-Saints.** Indian summer. Notice how perfect the description of this season is in lines 140–151 inclusive. The repose of Indian summer is so happily suggested by lines 143–148.

151. **Plane-tree.** A species of sycamore. The Oriental plane-tree "was much admired, and planted both by the Greeks and Romans as an ornamental tree — no other tree, indeed, commanding equal admiration; and for centuries the youth of Greece assembled under the shade of planes, in the groves of Academus and elsewhere, to receive lessons in philosophy."

The Oriental plane-tree grows as far East as Cashmere. "In those situations which are favorable to its growth, huge branches spread out in all directions from the massive trunk, invested with broad, deeply divided, and glossy green leaves. This body of rich foliage, joined to the smoothness of the stem and the symmetry of the general growth, renders the plane-tree one of the noblest objects in the vegetable kingdom. It has now, and had also of old, the reputation of being the tree which most effectually excludes the sun's beams in summer, and most readily admits them in winter, thus affording the best shelter for the extremes of both seasons. For this reason it was planted near public buildings and palaces, a practice which the Greeks and Romans adopted; and the former delighted to adorn with it their academic walls and places of public exercise. In the East, the plane seems to have been considered sacred, as the oak was formerly in Britain. This distinction is in most countries awarded to the most magnificent species of tree which it produces. . . . In the celebrated story of Xerxes arresting the march of his grand army before a noble plane-tree in Lydia, that he might render honor to it, and adorn its boughs with golden chains, bracelets, and other rich ornaments, the action was misunderstood, and egregiously misrepresented by Ælian (Var. Hist. II., 14)." — *Biblical Cyclopædia* (McClintock and Strong).

153. **Day with its burden and heat had departed,** etc.; i.e., the summer had departed.

154. **Brought back the evening star,** etc. What would the evening star be in autumn in Nova Scotia ?

157. **Foremost, bearing the bell, Evangeline's beautiful heifer,** etc. Compare this description of the heifer with descriptions of the doe in Wordsworth's *The White Doe of Rylstone.*

169. **Fetlocks.** The projection of a horse's foot above the hoof; also the tuft of hair on this projection.

190. Where was Normandy ?

190. Where was Burgundy ?

What great Norman is identified with the year 1066 in English history ? What great Duke of Burgundy was the contemporary of Louis XI. of France ?

192. **Spinning flax for the loom.** Representations of the spindle and distaff are to be seen on ancient Egyptian monuments.

The simile in 196, 197, and 198 is far-fetched. Longfellow's use of the simile was excessive.

204. **Settle.** A long seat with an upright back and arms. It is made of wood and is sometimes cushioned.

219. **Gaspereau.** A river of New Brunswick. In the treaty by which the French, in 1713, ceded Acadia to England, the limits of the territory thus named were not defined.

"The English claimed that Acadia ought to comprise all New Brunswick, besides the peninsula." — Edouard Richard.

230. **Louisburg.** When England and France were at war at intervals between 1689 and 1763, the colonists also took part. The first of the three intercolonial wars was "King William's," 1689–1697; the second was "Queen Anne's," 1702-1713; the third was "King George's," 1744–1748. In King George's war, the French lost

Louisburg on the island of Cape Breton. Louisburg at that time was called "the Gibraltar of America."

230. **Beau Séjour.** See Parkman's history, *The Pioneers of France in the New World.* "Beauséjour, Gaspereau, Grand-Pré, Beaubassin, Port Royal, sweet-sounding names, so full of memories, so familiar a hundred and fifty years ago, exist no longer except for lovers of history and antiquarians. Patient research is needed to find the spot where stood the village of Grand-Pré." — *Acadia* (EDOUARD RICHARD).

The hamlet of Gaspereaux is at the junction of the Gaspereaux and Salmon rivers.

230. **Port Royal.** For a graphic account of the founding, settlement, and loss of Port Royal, see Parkman's history. Port Royal was founded by Champlain and De Monts in 1605, in what is now Nova Scotia. The French lost Port Royal in King William's war. After the burning of Schenectady by the French and Indians, the English colonists, in retaliation, organized a successful expedition against Port Royal.

242. **Strongly have built them and well ; and, breaking the glebe round about them.** Let class analyze grammatical construction of second clause.

242. **Glebe.** Soil. In English history, church property in land is sometimes mentioned as glebe land. See use of this term in *The Nineteenth Century* (MACKENZIE).

244. **Inkhorn.** A receptacle for ink and made of horn; carried on the person.

247. **Blushing Evangeline heard the words that her father had spoken.** Is the comma at the end of this verse a better mark of punctuation than a semicolon would be?

III.

251. **Maize.** Indian corn. It is the most highly productive cereal known. It is an annual, and matures quickly. It thrives wherever the summer heat is intense. It grows in all parts of the United States, and in sheltered portions of Canada. The lands on the eastern shores of the Basin of Minas are among the most fertile and sunny in British America.

252. **Glasses with horn bows.** Spectacles, discovered in the

thirteenth century, were framed in horn or tortoise-shell till the beginning of the nineteenth century. Glasses with the horn or shell frame are now called goggles.

253. **Supernal.** "Of or pertaining to things above this world."

255. The rhythm in this verse is faulty.

258. What does this verse mean?

259. Paraphrase this verse in order to show the full force of *but*. With what verse does the action in this canto (III.) begin?

261. **Loup-garou.** Wehr-wolf; i. e., a ghost-wolf, — a wolf in human form.

275-276.   . . . **Evil intention Brings them here, for we are at peace; and why then molest us?**

During the French and Indian war, 1754–1763, the English became masters of the entire country east of the Penobscot. This tract included Acadia, which, however, had been previously ceded by the treaty of Utrecht.

Students interested in Acadia should read Parkman's version of their exile in *Harper's Magazine*, November, 1884. Parkman justifies their deportation. The opposite view is taken by Edouard Richard in his interesting work, *Acadia*. See vol. i., chap. iv.

The story of Evangeline was one of the traditions current among the Acadians after their dispersion.

The Acadians sailed away from Grand-Pré on Oct. 29, 1755. Edouard Richard says: "All that vast bay, around which but lately an industrious people worked like a swarm of bees, was now deserted. In the silent villages, where the doors swung idly in the wind, nothing was heard but the tramp of soldiery and the lowing of cattle, wandering anxiously around the stables as if looking for their masters. . . . The total amount of live-stock owned by the Acadians at the time of the deportation has been variously estimated by different historians, or to speak more correctly, very few have paid any attention to this subject. . . . Rameau, who has made a much deeper study than any other historian of the Acadians, sets the total at 130,000, comprising horned cattle, horses, sheep, and pigs."

Edouard Richard quotes the following from two contemporaries of the exiled Acadians: "The Acadians were the most innocent and virtuous people I have ever known or read of in any history. They lived in a state of perfect equality, without distinction of rank in society. The title of 'Mister' was unknown among them. Knowing nothing of luxury, or even the conveniences of life, they were content with a simple manner of living, which they easily compassed by the tillage of their lands. Very little ambition or *avarice* was to be seen among them; they anticipated each other's wants with kindly liberality; they demanded no interest for loans of money or other property. They were humane and hospitable to strangers, and very liberal toward those who embraced their religion. They were very remarkable for their inviolable purity of morals. . . . If any disputes arose in their transactions, they always submitted to the decision of an arbitrator, and their final appeal was to their priests." — MOSES DE LES DERNIERS.

"Young men were not encouraged to marry unless the young girl could weave a piece of cloth, and the young man make a pair of wheels. These accomplishments were deemed essential for their marriage settlement, and they hardly needed anything else; for every time there was a wedding the whole village contributed to set up the newly married couple. They built a house for them, and cleared enough land for their immediate needs; they gave them-live-stock and poultry; and nature, seconded by their own labor, soon put them in a position to help others." — BROOK WATSON.

296. **That a necklace of pearls was lost,** etc. Is *that* necessary to the sense? If not, why has the poet used it? Is the verse more or less rhythmical without the conjunction? See *English Versification*, page 9 (PARSONS).

308, 309. The simile in these verses conveys a vivid picture of how physical age may intensify expression.

311. **Tankard.** A large drinking-cup, sometimes with a cover. — *Standard Dictionary*.

325. What was the game?

The metaphors in 331 and 332 are among the loveliest in the whole range of Longfellow's poetry.

334. **Curfew.** Bell rung for the extinguishing of fires and lights. Supposed to have been introduced by William the Conqueror.

338. Before the time of matches, fires were carefully preserved in this way till morning. If it happened that, notwithstanding the precaution taken, the fire went out, another could be lighted only

by a spark struck from the friction of flint with steel, or by hot coals fetched from a neighbor's.

Does verse 315 contradict verse 347?

The custom of marriage dower is an ancient one. It existed long before the time of Solon. Among the Greeks, the dowery was settled upon the bride at the time of betrothal. Solon introduced a law to restrict the amount of a bride's dower. Plutarch gave as a reason for this law the danger the husband might suffer from loss of independence if his wife's dowery were too large. For these and further details on this interesting subject see Becker's *Charicles.*

Dante, in enumerating the sins of Florence in the *Divine Comedy,* says that her dowerless daughters remain unmarried.

350, 351. "On the days after new and full moon, the range of tide is as its maximum, and on the day after the first and third quarter at its minimum." — G. H. DARWIN, University of Cambridge.

Verses 356, 357, and 358 show the impressionability of sensitive youth to every passing influence.

Verse 361 subtly prefigures the future, perpetual exile of Evangeline.

Does it not seem in the first stanza of IV. as though the people were met together to discuss the English ships at anchor? This is one of the rare instances of ambiguity in order of thought of the poet, for among Longfellow's charms is clearness. The **feast of betrothal,** in the second stanza, removes, of course, from the reader's mind all possible doubt.

Verse 366 is finely expressive. Compare it with some of the more vigorous ones in *The Building of the Ship.*

368. **Came in their holiday dresses the** *blithe* **Acadian peasants.** Notice in Longfellow's translation of Dante's *Paradise,* Canto II., 26, 27, 28, the use of this word as descriptive of Beatrice.

"And the milkmaid singeth *blithe.*"
L'Allegro: MILTON.

369. **Jocund.**

" And the *jocund* rebecks sound."
L'Allegro: MILTON.

385. **Porch.** For nearness of the porch to the orchard see lines 66, 67.

386. In what respect does this verse resemble Homer?

391. **Glowed like a living coal when the ashes are blown from the embers.** The fiddler's aged face glowed with the fire and animation of youth.

> " Amid the strings his fingers strayed,
> And an uncertain warbling made,
> And oft he shook his hoary head.
> But when he caught the measure wild,
> The old man raised his face, and smiled ;
> And lighten'd up his faded eye,
> With all a poet's ecstasy ! "
> *Lay of the Last Minstrel:* SCOTT.

393. *Tous les Bourgeois de Chartres.* The citizens of Chartres. *Le Carillon de Dunquerque.* The chimes of Dunquerque.

394. **Anon.** Presently; soon.

One appreciates the poet's art in gathering the people for the betrothal, in order to have them on the scene as well for the king's message. Harmony, repose, pathos, compose the spirit of the poem. Its gentle tenor is not disturbed even by the bell and drum beat.

422. **Solstice of summer.** The 21st of June.

422–430 inclusive is a good illustration of a Virgilian simile.

In Colonial times, the church or meeting-house was used for all the public purposes of a community, as well as for religious services. There trials took place, and gatherings of the people for defence or counsel.

446. **Tocsin's alarum.** A signal sounded on a bell. In former usage, a drum used to sound a charge. — *Standard Dictionary.*

447, etc. The appeal of Father Felician transports us in feeling to the millennium, or backward to the Golden Age. Acadie becomes indeed Arcadia. But strength of judgment and sternness also are in the verse: —

> " Let us repeat that prayer in the hour when the wicked assail us."

Notice the musical arrangement of dactyls and trochees in verse 452.

472. **Emblazoned its windows.** To set off with glowing colors. To adorn with heraldic designs. Emblazonry is the collective term for heraldic devices. Heraldic terms are so often employed figuratively, as in the text of *Evangeline*, that the editor thinks it may be interesting and useful to both teachers and students to append a few

extracts from the valuable article on heraldry in the *Encyclopædia
Britannica:* —

"'Arms,' or 'armories,' so called because originally displayed
upon defensive armour, and 'coats of arms' because formerly em-
broidered upon the surcoat or camise worn over the armour, are
supposed to have been first used at the great German tournaments,
and to have reached England, though to a very moderate extent, in
the time of Henry II. and Cœur de Lion. To 'blazon,' now meaning
to describe a coat of arms, is the German 'blasen,' to blow as with
the horn, because the style and arms of each knight were so proclaimed on public occasions. The terms employed in heraldry are,
however, mostly French, or of French origin. Though now matters
of form and ceremonial, and subject to the smile which attaches to
such in a utilitarian age, armorial bearings were once of real use and
importance, and so continued as long as knights were cased in plate,
and their features thus concealed. At that time leaders were recognized in the field by their insignia alone, and these — both figures
and colors — because identified with their fame, from personal became
hereditary, were subject to certain rules of descent, and to the laws
of property and the less certain rules of honour. . . .

"The best, if not the only absolutely safe evidence for the origin
of armorial bearings, is that afforded by seals. Seals were in common
use both before and after the introduction of armorial bearings, and
they are not so likely as rolls of arms or monumental effigies to be
the work of a later age. . . .

"It is uncertain at what period armorial bearings found their way
into England. The Conqueror and his successors certainly did not
use them; they do not appear upon their seals, nor are they shown
upon the banners of the Bayeux tapestry. The monk of Marmontier,
probably a contemporary, describes Henry I., upon the marriage of
his daughter to Geoffrey of Anjou in 1122, as hanging about the bridegroom's neck a shield adorned with small golden lions, 'leonculos
aureos;' and, making mention of a combat in which Geoffrey was
engaged, he describes him as 'pictos leones præferens in clypeo.' It
is true that the number, attitude, and position of these lions on the
shield are not specified; but considering that not long afterwards two
lions became the arms of Plantagenet, and so of England, this may
fairly be taken as their introduction."

" Coats of arms were not at first strictly hereditary, nor even always permanent in the same person."

" Early bearings were usually very simple, the colors in strong contrast, and their form and outline such as could readily be distinguished even in the dust and confusion of a battle. They are mostly composed of right-lined figures, known in heraldry as ordinaries. The favorite beast is the lion."

" The earliest and most valuable records relating to English armorial bearings are undoubtedly the rolls of arms of the reigns of Henry III. and the first three Edwards."

" The colours in heraldry are : —

AZURE,	Blue, *asur.*	SAPPHIRE,	Jupiter.
GULES (rose),	Red, *gueules.*	RUBY,	Mars.
PURPURE,	Purple, *pourpre.*	AMETHYST,	Mercury.
SABLE,	Black, *sable.*	DIAMOND,	Saturn.
VERT (green),	Green, *sinople.*	EMERALD,	Venus."

" The blazoning by precious stones and planets, and even by the virtues, was a foolish fancy of the heraldic writers of the sixteenth century, and applied to the arms of peers and princes."

Some shields were covered with fur, others with metal, but within certain limits as to color.

478. **Ambrosial.** From ambrosia, the food of the gods (Greek); heavenly, fragrant, delicious.

" But when, at length, Jove set before them all things agreeable, to wit, nectar and ambrosia, on which the gods themselves feed, a noble spirit grew in the breasts of all." — *The Theogony :* HESIOD.

> " The goddess, speaking thus, before him placed
> A table, where the heaped ambrosia lay,
> And mingled the red nectar. Ate and drank
> The herald Argus-queller, and, refreshed,
> Answered the nymph," etc.
>
> *The Odyssey*, Book V.

Ambrosia " was brought by doves to Jupiter, and was occasionally bestowed upon such human beings as were the peculiar favorites of the gods. Ambrosia was also used as a fragrant salve, which the goddesses employed to heighten their beauty; with which Jupiter himself anointed his locks; and which had the property of preserving bodies from corruption." — *Chambers's Encyclopædia.*

481. This verse unites the motive of Evangeline's nature to that of Father Felician.

487. Notice the deep religiousness of this simile. Its force is increased when one remembers that the sun was an object of worship among the most ancient Greeks under the name Helios, that it was the emblem of the Egyptian god Osiris, and that it still symbolizes to the Parsees the god of light — the good — Ahurâ-Mazdâ.

497-500. Notice the cacaphony of these verses.

It would be well to read aloud the last stanza of IV. to better appreciate its beautiful rhythmical qualities.

v.

555, 556. Is there a repetition of thought in **refluent** and **fled away?**

557. **Waifs of the tide.** Waifs may signify anything carried by the wind or by the tides of the ocean; flotsam. Are **kelp** and **sea-weed** synonyms?

558-561. What is the rhetorical name of the sentence contained in these verses?

559. Define **leaguer.**

562-564. These verses suggest the Æneid.

577. **Like unto shipwrecked Paul on Melita's desolate sea-shore.** "And when they escaped, then they knew that the island was called Melita. And the barbarous people shewed us no little kindness: for they kindled a fire, and received us every one, because of the present rain, and because of the cold." — Acts xxviii., 1, 2.

577. **Melita.** "An island in the Mediterranean, on which the ship which was carrying the apostle Paul as a prisoner to Rome was wrecked." "Melita was the ancient name of Malta, and also of a small island in the Adriatic, now called Meleda." "Each of these has found warm advocates for its identification with the Melita of Scripture." — *Biblical Cyclopædia:* McClintock and Strong.

586-588. What word is ungrammatically used in this sentence? Is the sequence of tenses correct?

592. What book of the Old Testament and what character in that book had Longfellow probably in mind?

593-596. Is it the **moon** or the **light** which **Titan-like stretches its hundred hands?**

"But again, from Earth and Heaven sprung three other sons, great and mighty, scarce to be mentioned, Cottus and Briareus and Gyas, children exceedingly proud. From the shoulders of these moved actively one hundred hands, not brooking approach, and to each above sturdy limbs there grew fifty heads from their shoulders."
— *The Theogony*, HESIOD.

598. **Roadstead.** Places suitable for anchorage off shore, but without the shelter of a harbor.

601. **Gleeds.** Burning particles.

638–640. These verses are beautiful hexameters, and most poetic in thought.

Let the student notice how dramatically Longfellow has brought the first half of his narration to a close. His arrangement of subject-matter is such that Part the Second becomes an obvious and necessary division.

PART THE SECOND.

I.

3. **Bearing a nation, with all its household gods, into exile.** This is Virgilian. Anchises, the father of Æneas, when fleeing from Troy, bore in his hands the images of the household gods.

"There was a story (alluded to in one of the lost tragedies of Sophocles, of which we have but a fragment) that on the night of the capture of Troy the tutelary deities departed in a body, taking their images with them." — BLACKWOOD'S *Ancient Classics*.

The household gods of the Romans were called Penates; they were also named Lares, the two terms being synonymous. Jupiter and Juno, as protectors of domestic happiness, were Penates. Whoever left home prayed to the Penates and Lares for a safe return. To these household gods both the hearth and table were sacred.

7. Where are the **Banks of Newfoundland?**

9. **Savannas.** Meadow-lands.

10. **Father of Waters.** Mississippi = Missi Sipi = the Great Water.

11. **Seizes the hills in his hands, and drags them down to the Ocean.** "At the mouth of the river a large delta has been

formed by the mud and detritus carried down by the current. This delta is intersected by a number of outlets, or water-courses, called bayous, which issue from the Mississippi, or derive from it a supply of water in time of a flood. 'The whole area of the delta,' says Dana, 'is about 12,000 square miles.'" "'The new soil deposited in one year by the Mississippi,' says Guyot, 'would cover an area of 268 square miles with the thickness of one foot.'" — *Lippincott's Gazetteer*.

14. Is this verse grammatically correct ?

20. Is this verse a general statement, or does it apply exclusively to the Acadians ?

32. This verse is the subject of a well-known engraving.

40. **Coureurs-des-Bois.** Guides.

45. The accent on the first word of this verse must be vigorous, in order to read it smoothly.

48. **St. Catherine.** Probably an allusion to the St. Catherine, put to death in 307 A.D. by the Emperor Maximinus, after she was tortured on a wheel. Hence St. Catherine's wheel. St. Catherine is the patron saint of girls' schools.

51, 52. True philosophy.

54–62 inclusive. In this, as in all the scenes between Father Felician and Evangeline, there is a oneness of comprehension, growing out of the spirituality of their natures.

67. **Shards.** [Archaic.] 1. A broken piece of a brittle substance. 2. Any hard, thin covering or organ. Specifically: (1) An egg-shell. (2) A wing-cover, as of a beetle. — *Standard Dictionary*.

68–75 inclusive. These verses are the key to the treatment of the remainder of the story. I. of Part the Second serves as an introductory canto. It is balanced by the three stanzas which precede Part the First.

76. **Beautiful River.** Signification of Ohio.

77. **Wabash.** This river forms the boundary between Illinois and Indiana for nearly two hundred miles. It enters the Ohio at the south-western extremity of Indiana.

80. Replace the first word of this verse by another pronoun which will render the meaning clearer.

84. **Kith.** [Obsolete.] Friends, acquaintance. Used only now in the phrase, kith and kin.

86. Here we have an intimation that those two kindred spirits, Father Felician and Evangeline, had never been separated.

88. **Adown.** Poetical form. As a prefix (*a*) down has the force of from.

90. **Chutes.** A narrow channel with a free current, especially on the lower Mississippi River. — *Standard Dictionary.*

91. **Cotton-trees.** A species of poplar, valuable for its timber.

92. **Lagoons.** Bodies of shallow water at the mouths of rivers or connected with the sea.

93. **The wimpling waves.** A pretty alliterative picture of the calmness of the wash of the waves in a lagoon. Wimple. Ripple.

94. **Pelicans.** The common pelican is the size of a swan. Pelicans fly in large flocks. "The sudden swoop of a flock of pelicans at a shoal of fish is a striking and beautiful sight."

96. **China-tree.** A shade tree indigenous to India.

101. **Bayou of Plaquemine.** Part of the delta of the Mississippi.

103. **Network of steel.** What, probably, suggested this figure to the poet?

104. **Tenebrous.** Shady. This verse is composed entirely of dactyls and trochees.

105. **And trailing mosses in mid-air.** The long silvery gray mosses hanging in lengths of many yards from the live oaks in the cemetery of Bonaventura in Savannah, give a peculiarly solemn and cathedral-like aspect to the walks and drives under those huge trees.

107. **Herons.** The plumage of the heron is beautiful, though sober in color. The common heron builds its nest in lofty trees. Many varieties of this bird are numerous in the southern parts of North America.

111. **Gleamed on the columns of cypress and cedar sustaining the arches.** "The cedar proud and tall." "The cypress funereal." — Canto i., Book I., *Fairie Queen.*

Verses 111 and 112 complete the architectural picture of verses 105 and 106.

117. **Mimosa.** There are hundreds of species of the mimosa. Sensitive plants belong to this family. Some of the larger species are valuable for their timber, and attain the size of trees.

122. That is, Evangeline's view, after all, was but a phantom vision. The forebodings of her companions were true of their future.

132 *EVANGELINE.*

134. Notice the impressive simile in this verse.

136. **Canadian.** Is this word used in its modern geographical and political sense?

138. **Desert.** Is this word given its exact meaning?

142. **Atchafalaya.** This bayou is an outlet for the Red River, and also for the Mississippi. It is navigable by steamboats. It empties into the Gulf of Mexico.

144. **The lotus.** Here meant for a lily. Lotus is a Greek word, and besides applying to the famous Egyptian flower, also means a plant bearing a fruit useful for food.

146. Is this verse a true hexameter? Is it musical?

154. **Cope.** An arching cover.

141–158. This entire passage, if well read aloud, is euphonious and onomatopoetic. It produces the same effect obtained from reading aloud portions of Thomson's famous allegorical poem, *The Castle of Indolence;* especially those portions describing the "pleasing land of drowsy-head."

164. **Trappers.** Those who trap fur-bearing animals or game.

165. **Bison.** "The North American bison has light and slender hind quarters and densely shaggy fore parts. Commonly but less correctly called buffalo." — *Standard Dictionary.*

172. **Palmettos.** Any palm of the fan-shape. Here it means the cabbage-palm of the southern part of the United States.

177. **Tholes.** Fulcrums for the oars.

188. **Is as the tossing buoy, that betrays where the anchor is hidden.** Is this simile forcible?

191. **Têche.** Name of a bayou emptying into Atchafalaya bayou.

The last stanza of II. is exquisite. Notice the harmony of thought in the three pictures given: "**Sky and water and forest . . . melted and mingled together;**" "**the sacred fountains of feeling;**" "**shook from his little throat such floods of delirious music.**"

213. **Bacchantes.** Women who assisted in the worship of Bacchus. Their orgies partially consisted in frenzied dances.

III.

225. **Such as the Druids cut down with golden hatchets at Yule-tide.** The etymology of the word Druid is uncertain. The

Druids were the priests of the ancient Kelts. They taught the immortality of the soul. Among other subjects, they studied astrology and theology. Britain was their chief resort. They held the mistletoe in great veneration. The oak was their sacred tree. The mistletoe, though rarely growing on oaks, as it preferred such trees as the apple or pear, was, when found on them, revered for its magical qualities. When discovered on the oak, it was cut with a gold knife, by a white-robed priest, and two white bulls were sacrificed at once. In Druidic language, mistletoe signified All-Heal. The mistletoe, when growing on the oak, "represented man, a creature entirely dependent on God for support, and yet with an individual existence of his own."

225. **Yule-tide.** AS. Geól = December. The feast of mid-winter, the Yule, was sacred to Odin. Christmas-time.

249. **Sombrero.** A broad-brimmed hat.

Spain claimed, by right of discovery, a large portion of that part of North America included by the Southern States and the Pacific coast. It was in these regions the Spaniards made settlements. Through Napoleon's victories this section for a brief time became a French possession. In 1803, the portion then known as Louisiana, covering over a million square miles of land, and the whole length of the Mississippi, was purchased by the United States for $15,000,000.

Compare 260 with 308.

279. **"Be of good cheer, my child ; it is only to-day he departed."** This is the second highly dramatic combination of circumstances in the poem. Which was the first? Notice in the future development of the story whether there is an incident much like the one in verse 279, and, if so, whether the repetition weakens the force.

288. **Ozark Mountains.** Hills west of the Mississippi in Arkansas, Missouri, and the Indian Territory.

296. **Olympus.** Mountain in Greece. In Greek mythology, the home of the gods.

302. **While Basil, enraptured, hailed,** etc. That is, those who had accompanied Father Felician and Evangeline, and who were now coming up from the boat. Among them were those carrying Michael, who had gone down to meet his former companions, and also "the mothers and daughters."

305. **Ci-devant.** Former.

319. **Natchitoches.** A parish of Louisiana intersected by the Red River.

332. **King George of England.** George II. Date of reign, 1727–1760.

344. **It was the neighboring Creoles and small Acadian planters.** " Creole (Spanish Criollo) is a term which primarily was used to denote an inhabitant of the Spanish colonies who was descended from the European settlers, as distinguished from the aborigines, the negroes, and mulattoes. It is now more loosely employed, the name being frequently applied to a native of the West Indies whose descent is partly, but not entirely, European. A part of the colored population of Cuba are at times designated Creole negroes, in contradistinction to those who were brought direct from Africa. The Creole whites, owing to the enervating influence of the climate, are not a robust race, but exhibit an elegance of gait and a suppleness of joint that are rare among Europeans." — *Encyclopædia Britannica.*

360. **Heard she the sound of the sea,** etc. Interpret this sentence.

366–368 inclusive. The personification, metaphor, and simile are equally beautiful. These three verses are a fair illustration of the statement sometimes made that true poetry is the highest possible form of human speech, as in poetry the fullest thought can be packed into the briefest space.

379. **Upharsin.** Divided. Paraphrased, as in the Bible, Dan. v. 5–25, it means, "Thy kingdom is divided."

It would seem as though Longfellow must have used this term primarily for its musical sound, and secondarily, with some thought of the dispersion of the Acadians, and possibly as prophetic of the blight soon to settle on Evangeline's hope and search.

389. **Loud and sudden and near the notes of a whippoorwill sounded.** According to common superstition, it is a bad omen to hear a whippoorwill. To offset this, the poet adds the whisper of the oaks and the sigh of the meadow, which is a skilful way of expressing Evangeline's pathetic self-encouragement.

395. Explain the figure.

396. Explain **vases of crystal.**

IV.

The first stanza of IV. is a general description of the country immediately west and east of the Rocky Mountains, and the sections south of this region. Its very vagueness, while bearing an air of precision, is good art.

427. **Roebuck.** "The male of the roe-deer, a small deer of Europe and Western Asia." As Longfellow did not visit the scenes of *Evangeline* previously to writing the poem, he doubtless, in this instance, furnished the West with an animal suiting his fancy. He may have had in mind the Wapiti or American Elk, or the Antelope of the Rocky Mountains.

430. **Ishmael's children.** Meant here for nomadic Indian tribes. Ishmael was the son of Abraham and Hagar. Ishmael was not, as has been commonly supposed, the founder of the Arabian nation, for the Arabs existed before he was born. On his expulsion by Abraham, he joined the Arabs, adopting their nomadic habits, and eventually became the father of an important division of that people. Hence the term Ishmael has become synonymous with nomadic or wandering.

437. **Anchorite monk.** The term anchorite means one who has withdrawn from society. Anchorite monks were numerous in the Eastern church. They chose the wildest and most secluded localities, and were exceedingly austere in their habits, exposing themselves, scantily clad, to the roughest weather, and living on poor and meagre food.

439. **Like the protecting hand of God inverted above them.** A majestic simile.

440. **Fata Morgana.** A mirage peculiar to the Strait of Messina.

454, 455. The Shawnee Indians are a north-eastern tribe. The Camanches belong to the central plains of North America.

474. **And repeated the tale of the Mowis.** The legend suggests the story of Cupid and Psyche. For a beautiful poetical version of the Greek myth see *The Earthly Paradise* (MORRIS).

478–484 inclusive. These verses are as musical as some of Poe's famous lines.

No scene in the whole narrative better fits the ideas of remoteness and semi-human possibilities belonging to the aroma of true poetry than the one depicted in 472–498.

510. Saw the tents of the Christians, the tents of the Jesuit Mission. In *The Jesuits in North America*, the historian Parkman says, in speaking of Brébeuf and his associates: "Their patience, their kindness, their intrepidity, their manifest disinterestedness, the blamelessness of their lives, and the tact which, in the utmost fervors of their zeal, never failed them, had won the hearts of these wayward savages; and chiefs of distant villages came to urge that they would make their abode with them. As yet, the results of the mission had been faint and few; but the priests toiled on courageously, high in hope that an abundant harvest of souls would one day reward their labors." This was in 1635.

517. Notice the alliteration in **soft susurrus and sighs.**

524. Hearing, etc. What preposition is understood before *hearing?*

533, 534. Interpret the simile. Compare some of Longfellow's best similes and metaphors with those of George Eliot in *Silas Marner (Students' Series of English Classics).*

551–561. The gentle didacticism of the priest is so poetically expressed that even those critics whose creed is "Art for Art's sake" could hardly reject this intrusion, if it indeed be such.

564. Wold. A tract of slightly hilly country, usually unwooded.

576. Moravian Missions. The Moravians trace their origin to the followers of John Huss. They are Lutherans in their essential belief. Almost from the beginning of their history they were missionaries. Their first mission was established at St. Thomas, one of the West Indies, in 1732.

580–586. These verses mark the transition to the conclusion of the poem.

Is the beautiful metaphor in 585 weakened by the simile in the following verse ?

V.

592. Dryads. Wood-nymphs.

611–620 inclusive. Notice that every verse in this passage, which is descriptive of Evangeline's love for Gabriel as one lost on earth to be found in heaven, begins with a dactyl. It therefore embodies a twofold harmony, — the harmony of technique and the harmony of one fully developed thought.

638, 639. Analyze the meaning of these verses.

674. **And, as she looked around, she saw how Death, the consoler.** "The Angel of Death is the invisible Angel of Life." — HENRY MILLS ALDEN.

676. **Many familiar forms had disappeared in the night time.** One of the harrowing incidents to those who lose their dear ones in hospitals is that, when death occurs in the night, the bodies are at once removed.

The climax of the poem is reached in stanza fourth of Canto V. Longfellow's warm human sympathies are manifested in this conclusion; for *Evangeline* might have been drawn to a close with the passage included in 611–620.

All that follows after stanza fourth merely serves to relax the tension of feeling on the part of the reader. It is like the benediction after a sermon which has stirred a soul to the depths. It serves also to connect the end with the beginning, and thus complete the Acadian frame of a picture in ten cantos. Again, the three final stanzas harmonize with the three stanzas of the prologue, but with a reversal of arrangement, as befits the need of the poem.

ENGLISH LITERATURE.

Of our popular list of classics the editor of the Christian Union recently said : " *We cannot speak too highly of the Students' Series of English Classics.*" There are nearly thirty books now out and in preparation, and it is only necessary to read the list of our editors to gain an intelligent idea of the character of the work done. We do not add to this series for the sake of increasing the list, but we shall make the same careful selection of authors that are to come as we have in those announced. Any book announced in this series will be worth the attention of an instructor in English Literature.

Painter's Introduction to English Literature, including several Classical Works. With Notes.
By Professor F. V. N. PAINTER, of Roanoke College, Va. Cloth. Pages xviii+628. Introduction and mailing price, **$1.25**.

Morgan's English and American Literature.
By HORACE H. MORGAN, LL.D., formerly of St. Louis High School. A practical working text-book for schools and colleges. Pages viii+ 261. Introduction price, **$1.00**.

Introduction to the Study of English Literature.
In Six Lectures. By Professor GEORGE C. S. SOUTHWORTH. Cloth. Pages 194. Introduction price, **75 cents**.

The Students' Series of English Classics.
PRICES REDUCED. To furnish the educational public with well-edited editions of those authors used in, or required for admission to, many of the colleges, the Publishers announce this new series. *The following books are now ready*, and others are in preparation. *They are uniformly bound in cloth,* furnished at a *comparatively low price*, and Students of Literature should buy such texts that after use in the class room will be found valuable for the library.

LITERATURE.

Tennyson's Elaine . . . . **25 cents.**
    Edited by FANNIE MORE MCCAULEY, Instructor, Winchester
        School, Baltimore.

Macaulay's Life of Samuel Johnson . . . . **25** "
    Edited by GAMALIEL BRADFORD, Jr., Instructor in English
        Literature, Wellesley and Boston.

Scott's Lady of the Lake . . . . **35** "
    Edited by JAMES ARTHUR TUFTS, Phillips Exeter Academy.

Milton's Paradise Lost, Books I and II . . . . **35** "
    Edited by ALBERT S. COOK, Yale University.

Pope's Iliad, Books I, VI, XXII, XXIV . . . . **35** "
    Edited by WARWICK J. PRICE, St. Paul's School, Concord, N.H.

Longfellow's Evangeline . . . . **35** "
    Edited by MARY HARRIOTT NORRIS, Professor, New York.

Tennyson's The Princess . . . . **35** "
    Edited by HENRY W. BOYNTON, Phillips Academy, Andover, Mass.

The Following Volumes are in Preparation :

SHAKESPEARE'S MACBETH and AS YOU LIKE IT. Edited by
KATHARINE LEE BATES, Wellesley College.

GOLDSMITH'S VICAR OF WAKEFIELD. Edited by J. G. RIGGS,
School Superintendent, Plattsburg, N.Y.

DE QUINCEY'S THE FLIGHT OF A TARTAR TRIBE. Edited by
FRANK T. BAKER, Teachers' College, New York City.

CARLYLE'S ESSAY ON BURNS. Edited by WILLIAM K. WICKES,
High School, Syracuse, New York.

MACAULAY'S LAYS OF ANCIENT ROME. Edited by D. D. PRATT,
High School, Portsmouth, Ohio.

DRYDEN'S PALAMON AND ARCITE. Edited by W. F. GREGORY,
High School, Hartford, Ct.

LOWELL'S VISION OF SIR LAUNFAL, and Other Poems. Edited
by MABEL C. WILLARD, Instructor, New Haven, Ct.

We cannot speak too highly of the STUDENTS' SERIES OF ENGLISH
CLASSICS. — *The Christian Union.*

Correspondence invited.

LEACH, SHEWELL, & SANBORN,

BOSTON.   NEW YORK.   CHICAGO.